Blood Legs

Dan and Will Glass ride into Wyandot after a long, gruelling trail drive. But they are immediately drawn into a gunfight and from then on, nothing goes their way.

After the death of a powerful rancher, the brothers are arrested and locked up. The nervous townsfolk deem them to be members of a notorious gang of outlaws called the Blood Legs. There are signs that an ex-chain gang convict called Oleg Shine is the real leader. Were it not for the fact that he died long ago!

Threatened by a gullible and superstitious lynch mob, the brothers make a jail break and with some help from the gun lust of Cedar Truckle they set out to reveal the town's secret. Only then can peace return to the territory.

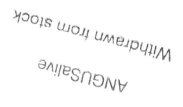

Blood Legs

CALEB RAND

A Black Horse Western

ROBERT HALE · LONDON

ISBN 0 7090 7588 X

Robert Hale Limited
Clerkenwell House
Clerkenwell Green
London EC1R 0HT

Typeset by
Derek Doyle & Associates, Liverpool.
Printed and bound in Great Britain by
Antony Rowe Limited, Wiltshire

1

THE BANK MEN

Flowing east, between the North and South Platte Rivers, Lobo Creek meandered through sand bars and flats. From where Dan and Will Glass sat their horses, the low banks were lined with willow and cottonwood.

Dan held his slouch hat against the sun, squinted at the town that was hazed by the shimmer of the land ahead.

'Don't look like the sort o' place that gives trouble,' he said to his brother. 'But that's what makes me nervous.'

Will gave a quick grin. 'Yeah, if you go more'n two days without it,' he agreed. 'For nearly a week you been on the peck.'

'Why'd you say that?' Dan bridled.

'Back in Pueblo, outside o' the pens, when we got paid off. You forgot?

'Nope. I took the money just like you did,' Dan answered back.

'Yeah, but I wasn't the one tellin' the trail boss he was a miserable, dried-up dung ball.'

Dan remembered. 'Goddamn cow pastor, paid us half what we earned. We're still owed,' he snorted.

'Forget it,' Will advised. 'That was another time, another State. Right now, we're takin' a break from driftin'.'

The hugger-mugger buildings of Wyandot lined both sides of a single street. Some tented, some false-fronted, a few Nebraska brick, but all weatherbeaten, and baked beneath the high sun.

The only person in obvious sight was a tight, nervy-looking man in dust-powdered range clothes. He was standing on the boardwalk that abutted the veranda of the town's bank.

Will was chary of the situation, didn't like the menacing way the man eyed them as they rode towards him. There were four saddle horses standing close by, but they were ground-hitched, standing ready.

Dan glanced quickly at Will. The brothers usually took in most of what was happening around them. In unfamiliar places it was a grounding that had often served them well.

'There's some gents must have a lot o' trust in their mounts,' Dan said. 'Either that or they're figurin' on goin' somewhere in a hurry. You notice they ain't tied in?'

Will leaned from the saddle, closer to his brother. 'That's cause they're robbin' the bank,' he said, out of the corner of his mouth.

'How'd you know that?' Dan asked, with an instant, incredulous smile.

'Can tell.'

Dan's eyes brightened with expectation. 'We gettin' involved?'

'No, an' don't stare. Keep ridin'.'

The two of them rode on down the street past the bank without even glancing further at the man on the boardwalk. But, sixty feet on, they heard a muffled shout from inside the bank building.

There was no doubting it was a distressed cry of shock. Will instinctively reined in his sabino, was twisting in the saddle when the hollow boom of a gunshot followed. The man on the boardwalk stepped forward quickly. His face twisted with anger as he reached for the reins that were turned around the saddlehorn of the nearest of the four horses.

'Leave them mounts,' Will challenged loudly.

'Suck dust,' the man yelled back. But he was panicked, fearful for his own hide and he made a grab for his handgun.

It was a mistake, and he howled with pain as a bullet from Will's long-barrelled Colt shattered his right wrist.

'Goddamn it. You said to keep ridin',' Dan said, swinging his own bayo mare in tight, testy circles.

'I suddenly thought there might be a reward.'

'We'd be best off stayin' alive,' Dan grunted his indignation.

Bothered at the shooting, the bank-robbers' horses stomped and snuffled. Three of them found there was nothing restraining them and whirled away, went tearing down the street in a panicky gallop.

Dan was watching them. 'You take the gunfight, Brother,' he shouted, before spurring off in close pursuit. The lookout's own horse tried to follow, but the stricken man dragged its bridle back with his good hand.

Three jittery men then dashed out of the bank. They were waving guns, probing for the expected trouble. Neck-cloths hid the lower part of their faces and their woolsey hat brims were bent down to mask their eyes. One of two men who carried a money bag, shouted furiously as he saw the retreating horses.

'You idiot, Bokse. You've let the goddamn horses get away.'

'Yeah, an' I got most o' my goddamn hand shot away.' The lookout man named Bokse, didn't try to explain further. He was having trouble enough holding on to his own mount.

At the sight of the masked men, Will sent his mare into a few big strides to cross the street. He swung from the saddle, jumped on to the rising steps of a saloon.

'Keep still, or you'll run into a bullet,' he muttered to his horse. Then he dropped the reins, pulled his Colt and ran to duck behind a stack of empty beer barrels.

Alongside him, a big man shoved himself out through the saloon's batwing doors. He carried a Winchester, was determinedly levering a shell into the breech. He leaned back against the clapboard wall, and raised the rifle to his shoulder. He took good aim at the nearest bank-robber, let out a judgmental curse and and pulled the trigger.

The rifle shot bowled thunderously into the street, and the masked man was lifted backwards as the big bullet hammered into his chest. He staggered back, but didn't go over. He took a sideways step, then forward, seemed to bow to an audience for the theatre. Then he dropped his gun and money bag, coughed and went down heavily to the dust of the street.

The guns of the other two outlaws started a frantic retaliation. Bullets split and fractured the wall planking behind the big man and he quickly leaped to one side, joined Will behind the barrels.

'How do,' Will said. He hunkered down, let himself topple from cover. Then he raised the Colt, and fired. The robber who was carrying the other money bag, crumpled with a bullet in his throat as he came down the bank's steps.

'Reckon we got 'em beat,' Will called out. But directly above him, the big man's rifle boomed again. This time the third bank raider got a bullet high in his leg. He kept going, but only to get shot again, fatally through his chest.

Bokse yelled, wild and fearful as he looked towards the aggressive gunfire from across the street. He saw the rifle in the big man's hands find him. Pathetically, he raised a shattered, bloody hand, tried to voice his surrender. But it was in vain, and the rifle crashed out for a fourth and final time, caught him somewhere low and vital.

'Murderin' scum,' he hissed, before throwing himself off the edge of the boardwalk.

Will heard the man's dying words, allowed himself a short moment of understanding. He stood up and thoughtfully turned the cylinder of his Colt, looked along the street to where he half expected to see his brother.

Alongside him, the big man slowly lowered his rifle. He tapped the barrel against the side of his leg, as if he was eager for more killing.

'He might have had a point,' Will said, indicating the dead man.

The big man started sizing up Will. 'He didn't have diddly squat,' he said glibly of the bank-robber. 'An' just who the hell are you, mister?' he asked.

'William Glass. Just passin' through, you might say. Who the hell are you?'

'I'm Cedar Truckle ... own this here Beaker's Brim.'

'Curious name,' Will suggested.

'The family owned a timber mill. My sister's name's Willow,' Truckle responded with a straight face.

'I meant the saloon,' Will said, similarly matter of fact.

'Oh, I see. Well, that's how they like it filled ... them that drink here,' Truckle said.

Will saw that the saloon keeper was baffled, maybe irritated. As though his interest had suddenly waned, he turned away because he'd seen a small crowd was gathering around the bodies in the street.

'Not what I'd call a profitable day's work,' Will suggested.

Will and Truckle stepped into the middle of the dusty street, where a heavy-set man with a sheriff's badge had started to take charge.

'That's Amos Hatte,' Truckle said. 'Old-time peace-keeper. He spent some years in Denver. Used to believe in a good beatin' when you rode in. Not on the way out.'

'Someone pick up them money bags. Take 'em back to the bank,' the sheriff rasped at the onlookers. Then he turned to look along the street, as Dan rode in leading the bank-robbers' horses.

'Here comes your partner,' Truckle said, his eyes watching Will for a reaction. 'Saw you ride into town together.'

'Yeah, I just bet you did,' Will said with a thin smile, not bothering to mention that Dan was his brother.

'In this town, I watch my neighbours,' Truckle said softly.

It was an ironic and obvious warning, and Will pondered on just how Truckle meant it.

'Anybody want these hay-bale mounts?' Dan shouted, having seen the sprawled figures. 'They'll not be needin' 'em. Not on the range they're ridin' over,' he added, a little more wistfully.

'Take 'em up to the sheriff's office. Leave 'em tied to the hitch rail,' Hatte ordered. 'I'll tend to 'em later.'

Sell 'em on as lawman's bonus, more likely, Dan thought, doubted the reward his brother had mentioned.

11

At that moment, Will noticed a man in a black frock coat standing in the doorway of the bank. He had a cadaver-thin face, and Will believed him to be casting a practised eye over the dead bank-robbers.

'From the boneyard, is he?' he asked Truckle.

'No. Well, yeah, sort of. He's Nestor Midland, owner of the Wyandot Bank. Listen up for some fittin' sentiment.'

'You people know that Cedar Truckle and me don't always see eye to eye,' Midland started off in stentorian manner. 'but when it comes down to keeping what's rightly ours, I back him all the way.' The banker looked at the gathering around him, dabbed a big handkerchief at his bony features. 'Yes, folks, thanks to him, the attempt to rob the bank of *our* monies has been a failure.'

'It was *my* money I was protectin',' Truckle muttered. 'Not yours or these goddamn pig farmers'.'

'Very public spirited,' Will muttered back.

'We got ourselves a wounded teller, inside,' Midland was continuing, 'but thanks to God *and* Cedar's prowess with a firearm, that's all.' Midland caught Truckle's eye, held out his hand in acknowledgement.

Truckle raised the tip of his rifle, nodded his head in return. 'This is where I could give you a mention, Glass, but I'm guessin' you ain't one for takin' advantage.'

'You guess right,' Will answered back. He had a sharp look around him, noticed how he'd caught the attention of two men.

True to form, Truckle had noticed them too. 'Rafer Vorn,' he said in a low tone. 'That's Elam Medows on the left. They ain't here to make friends, that's for sure.'

'I don't see why not,' Will laughed. 'All the other sort are dead.'

'They're never *all* dead,' the saloon owner advised drily.

2

THE SHORT SNAKE

With their curiosity sated, the small crowd drifted away. Will noticed that the two men Cedar Truckle had identified were among the first to leave.

Amos Hatte asked for the bodies of the four bank-robbers to be carried to the livery stable to await burial. The town had its own grave patch, a mile out of town in a fork of the creek.

'If I didn't know the truth of it, I'd say you had an interest in this town's undertakin' business,' Nestor Midland was saying to Truckle.

'If we had one, I would have,' the saloon keeper retorted.

Will strolled away. He'd picked up on the obvious bone of contention between the two men.

Dan was watering his mare at the trough, and Will collected his own mount. It was where he'd left it, out front of the saloon, long-suffering, with its reins still brushing the dust. The brothers then eased their saddles and led the horses further along the street, tied them to the hitch opposite the bank.

The sheriff stepped out from where he'd been asking questions of the wounded teller. He looked self-important, believed the town should be thankful for his continued safeguard.

'I'm Amos Hatte. So now you got the advantage,' he called out.

'Howdy Sheriff,' Dan responded. 'I'm Dan Glass, an' this here's my brother, William. But then our ma used to say that every like ain't the same.'

'An insightful woman,' said the sheriff, gave a pained, indulgent look as he approached.

'We're takin' on fluid. You want to accompany us?' Dan asked.

'Yeah. I'll buy,' Hatte offered. 'Call it a small reward.'

The three of them passed under the Beaker's Brim over-hang, the sheriff leading through the batwings. It was shadier inside, but not much cooler.

There was no sign of Cedar Truckle, only a handful of customers besides the barkeep. Will saw Elam Medows sitting alone at a table, skilfully riffling a deck of cards. The man named Vorn was drinking at the far end of the bar. Two other men were dressed plain, somewhere twixt shop-keep and Sunday style. They didn't appear much concerned by the sheriff, but Will knew that he and his

15

brother had already been deliberated for further trouble.

'Got a lemonade?' Will asked of the barkeep.

The barkeep pulled a brown bottle from a shelf, hooked the top off and pushed it towards Will. 'You don't get a glass with that,' he said.

'I'll take three fat fingers o' good whiskey,' Dan told him.

'Nothin' that's topsides, Ossie. Sheriff's reserve for me an' my friends,' Hatte instructed the barkeep.

From along the bar, Vorn turned and stared at the unusual exchange of words. Will downed his sweet, cloudy brew in a long pull and stared back. The drink was more than a thirst quencher. It was a calculated ploy to flush out the troublemaker, as there often was.

This time it was a little different. The man saw the icy challenge in Will's eyes, and considered for a moment. He eyed Will keenly, then turned and walked confidently from the saloon.

Will wasn't sure how he'd fared. He guessed it wasn't good for anything in the long term. Ah, what the hell, he thought, and smiled tolerantly at Dan.

The two other men, who still didn't appear to be too interested in the presence of the sheriff, made their way over to Medows' table.

'That couple's from the Short Snake. They work for Vorn,' Hatte informed Will and Dan.

The barkeep, who was always interested in the likelihood of friction, made his contribution. 'Like that feller Bokse. Him that was hangin' on to the horses. He tied in with Vorn about a week ago. That ain't much of a time, is it?' he reflected, unpleasantly.

'He's dead. An' that's a long time. If I was a town sheriff I guess I'd be usin' some lawful muscle to check that out,' Dan said with an optimistic edge to his voice.

Hatte smiled thinly. 'Well, you ain't,' he said.

'That's true,' Will said. 'See you sometime, Sheriff.' Deliberately, he tossed a silver dollar on to the counter to pay for the drinks.

The sheriff sniffed, offered up his glass for more whiskey, as Dan and Will walked away from the bar.

Outside of the saloon, Will waved his hand against the oppressive heat. 'We could've discovered who the sheriff's sidin' with,' he said.

'That's obvious,' Dan put in.

Will shook his head. 'Not necessarily. It looks like that, but like most lawmen, he plays his cards close to the belly. Any or either way, Brother, there's still a buck to be made hereabouts.'

Dan and Will didn't move straight along. Their attention had been drawn to three riders who were advancing from the other end of the street.

The man on the left had a big, white moustache beneath a big, beaked nose. He rode with an authority that clearly extended itself well into the town.

'Who'd you reckon the old beaver is?' Will asked, slow and thoughtful.

'Dunno,' Dan said, while noticing the quality of

the horses the men were riding. 'But he's *someone.* None of 'em are ridin' scrub meat.' He glanced the other way, along the street. 'Here comes your shoot-'em-up pard. Maybe he knows.'

Cedar Truckle nodded in acknowledgement as he reached the boardwalk. He took a step up, then turned and spoke out.

'You ought to gag that foreman o' yours, Fearon,' he growled at the hawk-faced man. 'I don't take kindly to bein' told what to do.'

'I'm sorry, Amos,' Fearon Chappel, said. 'He don't mean any harm. Not normally.'

Jasper Stebbs, the man Chappel was referring to, snorted contempt. The third rider, a younger, pale-featured man, stared fretfully at Fearon Chappel.

'Someone chidin' you don't have an easy goddamn ring to it, Pa,' he said.

'Don't upset yourself, Lester,' Chappel said quickly. 'Cedar an' me are old friends.'

'Yeah, like me an' buzzworms,' Dan said, out of the side of his mouth.

Will nodded in quiet thought. It was the second time he had stood by a personal, wordy exchange that involved Cedar Truckle.

It was just as he turned away that he saw the glint of metal from a rooftop on the opposite side of the street. Will saw the face, plain behind the sights of the rifle. In one movement, he stepped sideways, got support from a timber column, and made an instinctive move for his Colt. Within seconds, he'd fired off three shots, waited another to see if he'd need a fourth. A facia board at the top of the false-fronted building was holed, broken where his bullets had smashed their way through.

'What the jumpin' Jesus!' Dan exclaimed, with breathless awe. 'This dog town sure ain't lost any hair.'

The moment that Will had moved, he and Dan were covered by the guns of the three incoming riders. The men had reacted instantly, with the thought that it was them Will had been gunning for.

Will swore. But it was with some relief, because he noticed that Truckle was without his Winchester. The gun that had been fired earlier with such deadly effect was lying on the handrail fronting the saloon's veranda.

'What the hell game you playin', stranger?' Fearon Chappel's voice lashed out at Will.

'Someone's out to bushwhack one of us. Didn't have time to ask who,' Will explained. He nodded up the roof, opposite. 'I ain't got no enemies here, Mr Chappel. Not yet anyways. So. . . ?' Will let the implication hang in the air.

'You go find out, Jasper,' Chappel directed Jasper Stebbs. 'If there was someone, they'll have made back o' the street by now, so stay awake.'

'He's still up there,' Will said plainly.

Stebbs swung his horse across the street. He dismounted, looped the reins around the horn of the saddle.

A hinge of a batwing squeaked, and everyone turned to see Amos Hatte emerge from the saloon.

The sheriff was still holding five cards from his

game of poker. 'Now what?' he demanded gruffly.

'How much gunfire does it take to get your official interest, Sheriff?' Dan said drily, and before Hatte had a chance to speak further.

'Yeah it's been a long time since Denver,' Will added cuttingly.

3

THE LINK

From high on the building, Jasper Stebbs was looking down into the street.

'Don't know him, boss,' he called out to Fearon
Chappel. 'Looks like a 'breed.'

'Who shot him?' Amos Hatte's tone was curt.

'I did,' said Will. 'If I hadn't, he'da put down one
of us, here. Other than that, I really don't know
nothin'.'

'That's the trouble with this bear's ass of a place,'
growled the sheriff. 'Nobody knows much of
anythin'. An' a lot o' that's claptrap.'

Chappel and his son swung down from their
saddles, fastened their reins to the rail out front of
the saloon. Fearon Chappel strode over to Will and
offered his hand.

'Looks like I owe you, son,' he said. 'My name's
Fearon Chappel, own the Banded Wing. If you think
o' somethin' that would make good restitution, be

21

sure an' let me know what it is.'

'Yeah, goes for me too,' Lester Chappel said. 'What do they call you?'

'They call me, Will,' Will said. This is my brother, Dan. Lucky I happened to look up.'

'Well, if it weren't *you* boys, I can't think of anyone mad enough to ambush me in broad daylight,' Chappel senior suggested.

'I wager there's *some* who can,' Cedar Truckle laughed. Then he picked up his rifle and walked into his saloon.

Jasper Stebbs got back to the street. He picked out Will, and made straight for him. 'You shoot good, feller,' he commended. 'Two o' them bullets were high in his chest, less than a hand span between 'em. I'd say you ain't no cow-prodder.'

Before Will answered, Chappel was introducing Stebbs. 'Jasper's my foreman. Sometimes gets to trouble before I do.'

Will smiled impassively, watched Stebbs hand something to Chappel; something that was wrapped in a small, burlap square.

'He had this in his pocket,' the Banded Wing foreman said.

Chappel sucked air sharply through his teeth, turned a paler shade. 'That's a link from a fetter chain,' he said, then thought for a long few seconds. 'I thought the days o' the Blood Legs were over. Includin' Oleg Shine.'

'They are, Pa,' Lester Chappel said quickly.

Jasper Stebbs looked from Lester to his father. 'Now you get to wonderin', eh, boss?' he uttered, squinting back up at the roof top.

Chappel clapped his hands eagerly. Seeking escape from his thoughts, he went for his son's company. 'Nearly lost track o' what we came into town for, Lester. Let's go buy us some commodities . . . some comforts, maybe.'

Lester still appeared to be troubled as he followed his father. Stebbs had a quick glance at Will, who'd lifted a 'see you around' hand to Chappel.

'Don't anyone here bother; I'll get the body brought down,' Hatte said peevishly. Dan stepped closer to his brother. 'What's the hell's so worryin' about an old piece o' chain, Will?' he asked.

'Chappel went a little grey around the gills, when he saw it,' Will replied. 'I reckon findin' out might be interestin'.'

'That ain't the word I'd use, Brother. I'm for ridin' on.'

'Hmmm, perhaps we should,' Will said, with a thin smile. 'We'll think on it tomorrow . . . first thing.'

Dan made a move towards their horses. 'Good. I got myself a bad feelin' about this place,' he muttered to himself.

Will moved alongside. 'I'm kind o' curious though,' he said. 'Who an' what the hell's Blood Legs, an' their days bein' over? An' Cedar Truckle's sidewindin' his way in there somehow. Don't you think it's curious, Dan?'

Dan grabbed at his bayo's bridle. 'Not really,' he affirmed. 'Maybe if I was stayin', but I ain't. Let's get our horses put away . . . go see if we can get us some fixin's and some rooms.'

*

'An' I thought the old mad man o' the mountains was just a story,' Dan said.

The stable owner spat juice into the compacted muck of the yard. He grinned a mouthful of dark-coloured stubs. 'Thought I'd be seein' you two slicks sooner or later,' he rattled. 'Richmond Cord don't miss much that goes on in this town.'

'Good. We're goin' to put up for the night. Has Wyandot got a best place to stay?' Dan enquired amicably.

'It's usually out o' trouble.' The man grinned, his face squeezing into deep crinkles.

'Yeah, well, that ain't provin' easy,' Will said.

'I didn't miss that neither.' A pale eye widened, took a calculating appraisal of the brothers. 'The May Rooms is right down the street,' Cord went on. 'You can't miss it. It's the last building, the one with windows you can see through.'

'That's good as well,' Dan said. 'We'll say it came recommended.'

When Dan and Will entered the the double-fronted lodging-house, it was cleaner and more plushly furnished than either of them would have imagined. There were some comfortable-looking chairs and the place was aired and freshly painted. Bright curtains were drawn to the sides of its windows.

'Welcome, boys,' said the slender, fair-haired girl who stood watching them from behind a reception desk. 'I'm Ivy May, the proprietor of this establishment.'

'How'd you do,' Dan said. 'We been told you could fit us up with a couple o' rooms.'

The girl smiled. 'Mr Cord takes five per cent for every customer he sends over. If ever we get busy, that'll be more'n a top hand. We serve hot food, evenin's only.'

Will saw her look past him to one side, towards the door that had opened. He turned to see who it was that removed her welcoming smile.

The soberly dressed man who came in was one of a small handful of Wyandot folk whom Will would have recognized.

With the manner of someone who was in familiar surroundings, Elam Medows removed his hat, fixed his eyes on the girl. 'That 'breed who was gunnin' for Chappel? He was carryin' an iron ring,' he told her. Medows ignored Will and Dan, although he'd allowed them a sharp glance. 'I just heard about it in Truckle's place,' he continued. 'There's already talk about Oleg Shine comin' back.'

'Aah no, Elam,' Ivy shuddered, dropped the dipping pen she'd picked up. 'It can't be.'

'Let's hope not, Ivy. We don't want them days back,' Medows said dourly. 'I thought I'd best let you know.'

Ivy suddenly remembered that Will and Dan were waiting. They were still standing close, couldn't help but overhear. She turned to them, her eyes searching theirs for any sign of complicity. She was holding the keys to their rooms.

'I'm sorry about that,' she said, offering Will both

keys. 'One's a corner room, looks back along the street. Don't forget, supper's at eight sharp.'

4

THE CROSS RIVERS

Will knew that Elam Medows was watching him and Dan. The man who Cedar Truckle said wasn't for making friends, was leaning against the desk, and he suddenly appeared to be interested. As the brothers headed for the stairs, he took a couple of steps towards them.

'You boys hold up there a moment,' he called out.

Will and Dan exchanged a wary look with each other as they stopped and turned. 'You talkin' to us?' Dan asked.

'You ridin' on, or you aimin' to stick around?' Medows asked.

'Don't see it's any business o' yours, either way,' Dan told him.

'It's a curious question, mister. You tryin' to railroad us?' Will matched his brother for lack of guile.

'No, not me, boys. I've seen your funnin' around in the street. As you say, it ain't my business, but there'll be *somebody* wonderin' what your plans are.'

Will eyed the man with a testing glare. 'Well, it can only be a friend o' that 'breed rifleman, or Vorn, for *one* reason or another,' he retorted coldly.

'Well, as I said, I ain't got no personal interest. I'm sure Ivy don't want no trouble brought over here.'

Will and Dan watched as Medows tipped the brim of his hat to Ivy and made to leave. Will was going to say that any further trouble wouldn't be of their making. But it seemed pointless, so he didn't.

He went on up the stairs and, after a long suspicious look behind him, Dan followed. There was carpeting beneath their feet, little sound, save for the concho on one of Dan's spurs. They found their rooms and Will put the key into the lock.

'Real considerate o' that dude to warn us off,' Dan said.

'Yeah, weren't it just. Gets me to wonderin' what the hell's goin' on around here.'

'I told you before we rode in, I didn't like the look o' this place,' Dan muttered unhappily.

Will turned the key and pushed the door open. 'You're goin' to like this even less,' he said, staring down at the man, spread-eagled on the floor. There was a long tent peg angled out of the man's lower belly and a rusty chain link was clenched between his teeth. 'The lady's given us the keys to a room with a goddamn stiff lyin' in the middle of it,' he said broodingly.

Dan hissed a thin sound of astonishment as he moved past Will into the room. 'Sure didn't seem the kind,' he said, kneeling beside the body. 'Whoever this is, he's colder'n a witche's ass.'

'Pretty effective killin'. He's still wearin' his gun,' Will pointed out.

Dan looked up at his brother, saw the door of the room closing quietly. 'Will,' he called out. 'The door . . . someone's closin' it.'

Behind Will, the door pulled to. The key clicked, quickly twisted the lock in its housing.

Will turned and made a grab for the handle, pulled futilely. 'Too late, we're goddamn locked in.'

'Medows. It's got to be him,' Dan said. 'But what the hell for?'

'The sheriff'll probably give us a reason, if we stay here,' Will reasoned.

'Yeah. An' I don't like bein' shut in. Never did,' Dan said, moving to face the door. He considered for a short moment, then punched the heel of his boot hard against the door stile. With a grating split, the wood gave way and the door immediately broke open.

Dan drew his Colt. 'Let's go,' he said.

But Will held up his hand. He quickly rifled through the dead man's clothing, eased his fingers into a bloodstained pants pocket. 'Wouldn't you like to know who we're supposed to have killed?' he asked his brother. He withdrew an envelope, opened it where it had been double folded. The stamp and postmark had been torn away, but it carried the address: *Joseph Dace. Cross Rivers Ranch. Lobo Basin. Nebraska.*

Dan stepped back cautiously from the landing into the open doorway.

'Reckon I shouldn't be readin' dead men's mail, Dan,' Will said, 'but if this here's Joseph Dace, he sure ain't goin' to mind. Listen to this.

Dear Joe. Remember what we thought was our Thanksgiving present for them Blood Legs? We thought we sent Oleg Shine to his grave – well, we didn't. Now, like he said, he's seeking us out. So you got to stay on watch, Joe. I trust you are well.

Your old amigo, Garney C.

'Looks to me like this Oleg Shine feller's already got here,' Dan said. 'I wouldn't care much for someone who put me out on the big trail, either. Does all o' this throw any light on your wonderin', Will?'

'A thin, early-mornin' beam, maybe. You know, before we leave town, we got to find out who stuck this man.'

'Er, why?'

'Because now we're caught up. That dead man in our room weren't a chance thing. It was meant to be. If we ride out now, think how it would look.' Will shoved the letter into his own pants pocket. He picked the chain link from the man's mouth, and, frowning, looked at it closely. Then he put that too, in his pocket.

'Let's just get out of here, before someone turns up,' Dan said.

Both men walked back down casually to Ivy May's desk. She was talking to a sun-wrinkled oldster who was chuntering on about the coach from Wyandot.

'Got a feelin' I won't be needed for much longer,' he drawled. 'Hear the railroad's goin' to run a spur line out from Julesburg.'

'I wouldn't worry yourself about that, Jehu,' Ivy May said. 'By the time that happens, we'll all be retired.'

Will put the room keys on the desk top. 'Seems like somebody got to one o' them rooms before us, ma'am. They're sleepin' real sound, too,' he said calmly.

Ivy May looked surprised. 'I'm sorry. I don't know how that could have happened. There's two other rooms at the back. They overlook the trash cans, but if you want. . . ?'

'Yeah, they'll do just fine, ma'am.' Will thought that Ivy looked duly taken aback. If she knew there was a dead man upstairs, it was a good response.

'Room four. Five leads off,' she said, with a slightly perturbed smile.

'I was just wonderin',' Will said casually, as he took the new keys. 'A while back, we met up with a feller named Joe Dace. Said he could find some work for us. You heard of him?'

'Why, of course. Most people along the creek know of Mr Dace. He owns the Cross Rivers. He was here last night, but I was told he left this morning at first light.'

'I think you were told wrong, lady,' Dan said softly.

'How do you mean?' Ivy asked.

'He don't mean nothin',' Will said with a quick, stuttering laugh. 'He's seein' things . . . fevered from lack o' vittles, I guess. He swears he saw old Joe

playin' mumble-peg with a jackass in the middle o'
the street.'

Ivy's perturbed smile became more uncertain, as
Will clapped his brother on the back.

5

THE OUTCASTS

Talking earnestly and loud, Amos Hatte, Rafer Vorn and Cedar Truckle strode into the May Rooms together.

Dan and Will were standing with their backs against the reception desk. They watched with disguised interest as the three men walked up to them.

'Just got down here in time, it seems, Brother,' Dan muttered, out of the side of his mouth.

'Where is he?' Hatte, demanded. 'What did you do with him?'

'Did what with who?' Will enquired, against the sheriff's aggressive manner.

'Joe Dace. I hear one o' you two's just done him in.'

'Mr Dace isn't here,' Ivy said, quickly. 'There's been no one in, except Elam Medows. He only came to tell me about—'

'That's just it, Ivy,' Vorn interrupted. 'We reckon the Blood Legs have rose up. It was Elam told us about Joe Dace's killin'.'

'Before you go makin' any real blunders, perhaps you better listen to what we got to say,' Will addressed himself to Sheriff Hatte.

'Go ahead, say your piece,' Hatte said.

'We've seen the body. It was in one o' the rooms Miss Ivy gave us the keys to,' Will answered. He glanced at Ivy, who gasped audibly, shook her head. 'The man was stabbed, but you'll see it weren't with a knife. I can tell you who we reckon did it . . . the way it looks. We already heard the name mentioned once or twice . . . Oleg Shine.'

'Mr Dace left here this morning,' Ivy stuttered, the blood already drained from her fair face.

'No, ma'am,' Dan told her. 'He ain't been nowhere, 'cept that room upstairs.'

'Where the hell you get the notion it was Oleg Shine, mister?' Truckle demanded.

'He mean somethin' to this town, does he? To you?' Dan asked bluntly.

'He was a murderin' horse-thief. An' last fall, he got hung for one. I remember his last words . . . all those of us who was there, do. He said he'd be back.'

'Ghost rider, was he?'

'Maybe. Them Blood Legs were mostly long-termers. Lifers, some of 'em. They were a bad bunch, joined up with renegade Foxes an' Sioux.'

'I told you no good would come o' that night,' the sheriff said. 'There never was any proof, an' you all knew it.'

'It was Thanksgiving, and my pa was there,' Ivy put in. 'There wasn't much guilt; he told me so, but he had to live with it.'

The sheriff turned to Vorn. 'An' I'm kind o' curious as to why Medows should be creatin' a tale for you,' he said. Then he spoke to Will. 'Cedar asked why you're fingerin' Shine?'

Will pulled Dace's note from his pants pocket. 'I found this on the body. Thought I might need it, if things turned chancy.'

While Hatte ran his eye over the note from Garney C, Will told of what happened when he and Dan had gone up to check in.

'You said there was someone sleeping in one of the rooms,' Ivy said, noticeably confused.

'Sorry ma'am. I exaggerated a bit,' Will responded. 'We thought you might have set us up.'

'How'd you know she didn't?' Hatte asked.

'The lady told us that Dace had left early. I believed her,' Will said.

'Why don't you speak to whoever it was told her the lie?' Dan added.

'I will,' Hatte muttered. Then he thought for a moment, and handed the note to Truckle. He looked from Dan to Will. 'The man who wrote that's Garney Coddle,' he explained. 'He used to be Joe Dace's foreman at Cross Rivers.'

Truckle looked up. He shuddered. 'Looks like a goddamn spook's after us.'

'It's all hokum. Let's go see what's upstairs,' Hatte said. 'You comin', Cedar?'

'No. I'll give these two fellers a grasp o' Shine and

his people. They've a right to know.'

'I think I ought to have gone with the sheriff,' Ivy said. 'Perhaps he'll need the door key.'

'No. I don't think he. . . ' Dan started to say, but thought better of it.

'Who is this Oleg Shine that's causin' such a hulla-baloo?' Will asked Truckle.

'That's what I was goin' to tell you. It's an odd story. They were all ex cons. Got 'emselves amnestied from Fort Lincoln, an' a couple o' hard-labour Pens along the Lower Missouri. One or two came into town, but mostly they kept to 'emselves. They exchanged their calicos for store-bought duds, moved into the old swing station north o' Lake McConoughy. Oleg Shine was their leader, their chief o' staff.'

'Why are they called Blood Legs?' Will wanted to know.

'The shackles they wore. Took away flesh above the ankle.'

'That's mighty interestin'. But none of what you've said leaves 'em outside o' the law. Not from a State Pardon,' Dan observed.

'A buddy o' mine up in Scottsbluff says a gang o' yardbirds are sellin' to him. Most of the stock have burned brands, but he don't ask too many questions. He buys 'em bottom dollar, as they run.'

'An' that's how you tie in Shine and the others?'

'Yeah. Between here an' the Platte there's four ranches: Fearon Chappel's Banded Wing, Nitch Gordam's Long G horse ranch, Joe Dace's Cross Rivers, an' Vorn's Short Snake. From spring through summer last year, they was all losin' stock.'

'Vorn was losin' stock?' Will queried.

'Plenty. Why'd you ask?'

'He was quick to point the finger o' suspicion our way. I'm just givin' back some. He's also employin' some unlikely-lookin' cowpokes.'

Truckle was about to continue with the story, when an excited youngster pushed his way through the front door.

'I got to find Amos Hatte,' he gasped. 'They told me he was here.'

'Steady on, kid. What's the problem?' Truckle asked.

'There's some big trouble, Mr Cedar,' the boy went on hurriedly. 'Some riders came at us this mornin'. They was wearin' some sort o' white masks. They shot two of our boys, set fire to one o' the hay barns, an' stole some saddle-brokes we was takin' to Leavenworth. Where's the sheriff? I got to tell him.'

'I'm here, Albie,' Hatte called out, as he came lumbering back down the stairs with Vorn and Ivy May close behind him. 'What's happenin?'

'Mr Gordam's bristlin' bad, Sheriff. He said to bring you out fast as I could.'

'He shoulda said, as fast as *I* could,' Hatte retorted, and hitched up his broad gunbelt.

'Them riders were wearin' execution hoods. Sort of a telltale mark,' Truckle said, agitated and plainly nervous. 'There was a time when they'd come in whistlin', when they wore them iron rings as toggles for their neck scarfs. Perhaps Oleg Shine's got back with his ex-cons.'

It seemed to Will that Truckle's response to Oleg Shine was close on irrational. He couldn't understand how a man who'd stood his ground to gun down a gang of bank-robbers, could be so fearful.

6

THE PASSING APPEARANCE

A soon as Amos Hatte heard young Albie's story, the lawman got himself a bunch of riders together. Will and Dan, Cedar Truckle and Rafer Vorn were among those who rode with him to the Gordam horse ranch.

'I wasn't one of them who tried to stretch his neck. Why should Oleg Shine come for me?' demanded Nitch Gordam. 'Are these Blood Legs plannin' to raze everythin' twixt big rivers, because o' that Wyandot lynch mob?'

'Maybe. I don't rightly know,' Hatte replied. 'But lookin' at things all round, I figure we're in for plenty o' trouble.'

'You rode all this way to tell me that?' barked Gordam. 'What the hell do you get paid for, Sheriff?'

'I know how you must be feelin', Nitch,' Hatte said, taking up the sting of Gordam's wrath. 'I came to tell you we're goin' after 'em. An' this time, the job'll be done right.'

It was early dusk when the sheriff spurred his horse away from the ranch. He seemed to ride with purpose, but after two hours, Dan suspected that he might not be too certain as to where the outlaws might have gone.

'Pretty soon, we'll be ridin' up our own asses,' he said to Will.

Cedar Truckle overheard, and had the same idea. 'We're runnin' these mounts into the ground, Sheriff,' he grumbled. 'Admit it: there ain't no trail, an' you don't really think they headed back to Lake McConoughy, do you?'

'Don't know. Where else they goin'? They ain't exactly welcome as long-lost cousins in these parts,' Hatte conceded.

When others sided with Truckle, the sheriff reluctantly agreed that his unofficial posse might as well head back. The men gave each other an appreciative look in the near full dark, turned their horses to Wyandot.

When Will and Dan walked into Ivy May's dining-room it was long gone eight o'clock, but for obvious reasons, the evening meal was still under way. Vorn and two of his men were already seated at one table. Truckle and Medows were at another, on the opposite side of the room.

'You know what?' Dan said. 'All of a sudden, I got

40

me a desire to hurt that goddamn Medows. I ain't forgot it was him that put the word out it was us killed Joseph Dace.'

'I ain't too convinced o' that Dan, an' nor should you be,' Will said quietly. 'Vorn could o' been lyin'. An' given a choice o' the two. . . ?'

'Yeah, I know what you mean.' Dan understood his brother's hanging intimation. He looked across at the Short Snake rancher. 'He ain't got an honest face.'

They took a table in the near corner, and Dan slid into a chair facing his brother.

'Hatte ain't agin' us, either. Well, not any more he ain't,' Will said. 'I talked to him when we were ridin' back to town. He knew we couldn'ta killed Dace.'

'How'd he know that?'

'The man was a stiff as a post, that's how. Sheriff figured he'd been dead since the early mornin'.'

'Did he ask about the night clerk tellin' Ivy May that Dace had checked out at first light?'

'Don't think he had time to see him before we all rode to Gordam's,' Will said. 'But it's sure one thing I'd like to know about.'

Across the room, Vorn rose from his table. He walked determinedly to where Will and Dan were sitting.

'You two are rufflin' my feathers,' he said testily. 'If you got somethin' to say, say it.' The man gripped the butt of his gun to show his rough purpose.

Will sat motionless. Vorn's face clouded, the doubt showing once again.

'I reckon you should keep your mouth buttoned, mister, until you're real sure o' your ground,' Dan suggested calmly. 'In the meantime, I'll talk about anybody I choose. You savvy?'

At that, Vorn grabbed down at Dan's collar and dragged him up and out of his chair. But Dan was ready. He'd goaded for the move, and his boot heel was already crunching into Vorn's toes. He twisted his body and bunched the knuckles of his right fist sharply into the side of Vorn's face. Then he hit him hard and low in the belly with a short left.

Dan stepped back as Vorn crumpled slowly at his feet, at Ivy May's timely appearance in the dining-room doorway.

'You put that gun away,' she immediately snapped at Will, who'd all the while had Vorn's table covered.

Then Vorn scrambled to his feet. The lower half of his face was raw and snotty, his manner incensed with rage and humiliation.

'He might have wealth and influence, ma'am, but he'll still give your place a bad name,' Dan said, with a smirk.

'It's the sort of behaviour best kept for the back alleys. Yours, too, I might add, Mr Glass,' she reproved.

Dan nodded contritely. Will grunted and thrust his gun back in his holster.

'It was all down to Vorn, Ivy,' Cedar Truckle, called out. 'Got to say though, neither of 'em were too long on etiquette.'

'I was hungry. Didn't even get to the list o' fixins','

Dan said, with a gleam of anticipation as he reseated himself.

One of Vorn's cowboys took his hat from the rack. He handed Vorn his, and all three Short Snake men headed for the door.

Will watched them leave, then got to his feet. 'We're truly sorry, ma'am,' he said. 'But like Mr Truckle says, Vorn was actin' mean an' proddy. If Dan hadn'ta defended himself, there's no tellin' where it would have all ended.'

Ivy gave the brothers a stern look, but the anger had faded. Then she turned and walked back out of the room.

Will sat down again, kept his eye on Elam Medows as he followed Ivy. He'd already noticed that Ivy held more than a passing interest in the card player, and for some reason, found himself not liking it.

'Now I got me a trapper's gut,' Dan rumbled, as he looked pleasurably at the checkered tablecloth and shiny cutlery.

Nearly an hour later, Cedar Truckle went to pay for his meal. He stopped and looked at the Glass brothers as he went by their table.

'If you're also lookin' for trouble, you got to wait 'til I finished my cobbler,' Dan said, twisting the bowl of his spoon into the warm fruit.

'No, not me,' Truckle smiled. 'Do you mind if I draw up a chair? What I got to say won't interrupt your eatin'.'

Will nodded that it was OK, and Truckle got himself a chair and sat down.

'Elam Medows didn't accuse you o' killin' Joseph

Dace. He's just told me he didn't even know about the murder. Vorn was lyin' when he said Elam told him.'

'I wonder why that don't surprise me,' Will said uncaringly. As he spoke, he looked beyond Truckle. An extraordinary unease made him tremble when he saw the shadowy figure who'd appeared in the doorway. It was a tall, spare man with close-cropped grey hair. The man stood very still, his dark eyes holding Will's for a moment, as he quartered the room. Then, as ephemerally as he'd appeared, he turned and was gone.

'This Oleg Shine we been chasin'. He'd be some sort o' fool to ride into Wyandot,' Will suggested thoughtfully.

'The man's a big passel o' things, but plum stupid ain't one of 'em. Anyways, he'd be smelled out before he crossed the Lobo.'

'If you say so,' Will conceded.

'Well, fellers, I got to get goin',' Truckle said, pulling on his Stetson. 'There's night business at the Brim to take care of.'

Truckle acknowledged Dan as he looked up from the last of his meal, then he walked from the room. Outside, he hesitated on the raised boardwalk and sniffed at the night air. He flexed his shoulders and gave a thin smile, strode on briskly towards his saloon.

'When I've got me some coffee, there's somethin' I got to tell you,' Will told his brother.

7

THE NIGHT RAID

When Will and Dan had eventually finished their meal, deliberated recent events and likely outcomes, the May Rooms appeared to be deserted. There was no sign of Elam Medows and Ivy, or of the stranger whose identity Will had speculated on.

'You still got them other room keys, Will?' Dan asked.

'I have, an' I'm getting' mighty close to usin' 'em. I wonder if the sheriff found a chance to question the night clerk?'

'Who cares?' muttered Dan. 'Like you, I'm busted.'

They didn't see or hear anyone as they made it to the upstairs landing. Will unlocked the door to room four, lighted a lamp and quickly looked around the room.

'Anyone in yours?' he called out a moment later.

'Only me,' a relieved Dan answered from the adjoining room, as Will pushed the door to behind him.

The brothers had been more than an hour into their respective sleeps, when a band of horsemen entered the western end of Lobo Basin. They rode across the fertile grassland, circled places where tight stands of cottonwood choked a more direct route.

Their leader was mounted on a heavily muscled grey at the head of the line. When they'd travelled a few miles, he held up his hand to signal a halt.

'Like I told you, the first four's to head for Wyandot. Follow the creek, an' wait there for the signal,' he said curtly.

'We still don't know what's for the rest of us, boss,' one of the other men said, as the column bunched.

'With me, to the Banded Wing,' the big man told him. 'Fearon Chappel's got a herd readied for Cheyenne, an' they're pullin' out at first light. But I've got a special task for you, Deepdish,' he added.

'What's that, boss?' Lew Deepdish asked. 'Somethin' more satisfyin'?'

'There's some'd say so. I want you to despatch a couple o' packages.'

'Ha, that's better. Sendin' saddles home in a feed-sack, eh, boss?' Deepdish said, confidently. 'Who are they?'

'They're brothers, called Will and Dan Glass. They're put up at the May Rooms in Wyandot.'

'Yeah, I know it. An' I've heard o' them, too.' But Lew Deepdish suddenly didn't sound quite so sure of himself. 'The one that brought down the 'breed this mornin's some curly wolf.'

'You sure you're up to it, Lew? Tell me now if you ain't.'

'I ain't lived this long by not bein' appreciative of a good gun, boss. I'll need to take 'em in my own time.'

'Good. Just make sure that's within the next day or so,' boss man insisted.

Deepdish raised his hand in response, swerved his horse away across the creek towards Wyandot.

Out on the Banded Wing, the lone nighthawk was murmuring a few bars of 'Leaving Cheyenne', as he circled the bedded-down herd. The weary cowboy didn't see the shadowy figure that appeared from the stand of gnarled willow, the fleeting gleam on the blade of a skinning knife.

'You ain't even goin' to make Cheyenne,' the rustler mocked, as he leaped silently from the ground. The fingers of his left hand clutched at the rider's neck, his right plunged the knife upwards, deep into the nighthawk's side.

The plaintive notes of the dying man's song broke into a stuttering gasp as he slid from the saddle, twisted heavily into the hard ground.

The rustler gave a sharp whistle, and almost instantly, horsemen appeared from the darkness to surround the herd.

'Get the goddamn horse,' the big boss man called. 'If it gets back, they'll send out guns.'

A rider kicked his horse after the nighthawk's mount, while others moved through the herd, urging the cattle into motion. Within twenty minutes, they were gone, running west towards Pine Bluffs and the borders with Wyoming and Colorado.

Back in Wyandot, in the early hours, Will suddenly opened his eyes. He'd only been half asleep, but something brought him fully awake. First, there was a scuffling sound from around the trash cans below his window, then muffled thumps from somewhere further into the town. 'Dogs an' drunks,' he affirmed, and swore silently, returned to his broken slumber.

It was nearly eight o'clock, when he appoached Ivy May. Her fair hair was catching the early light, as she busied herself with papers behind her desk. Her smile was genuine, but slight, and there was nervousness in her manner.

'Good mornin'. Did you sleep?' she asked, tentatively.

Will thought for a moment. 'Well, now you mention it, ma'am, I did get sort o' disturbed. It was someone either turnin' in late or risin' early. Couldn't tell which.'

Ivy shook her head. 'It was marauders. They're sayin' it was the Blood Legs.'

'Where?' Will asked.

'They broke though the rear of the bank, as well as the hardware store for boxes of ammunition. An' they took in Harrison. Stole a herd from the Banded Wing, too.'

'Phweeew. They spread 'emselves around a bit,' Will said, partly in admiration. 'I'd like to know what Fearon Chappel thinks is goin' on.'

'Well, why don't we take a ride out there and ask him?' Dan said, still buckling on his gunbelt as he came into the room.

'Mornin',' said Ivy. 'You won't be welcome. Mr Chappel's been actin' strange lately. He don't welcome visitors.'

'Since he last came to town, no doubt,' Will said. 'My brother's right; I guess we'll try it anyway. The man knows I ain't his enemy.'

'Of course. I'll be here,' Ivy said, and gave a smile that Will took a liking to.

'Yeah, well, me an' Dan'll grab us somethin' down the street. We'll see you later, ma'am,' he said, amiably.

As Will and Dan left the May Rooms, they paid no attention to the hard-faced man wearing a bleached duster, who stood back on the planked walk.

Covertly, Lew Deepdish watched the brothers until they turned into a narrow-fronted beanery for their late breakfast. After a moment or two, he went for his horse and swung lazily into the saddle, rode slow and mindful from the town. He was thinking about Oleg Shine's demands, and had some planning to do, knew he had to be real careful.

Will and Dan ordered up two wax-paper packages of bread, bacon and cold eggs when they'd finished their ribsticker breakfast. Then they headed for the livery stable, where Richmond Cord was sitting out front, slicing a fresh chaw of Brown Mule.

'You two buckos found more trouble yet?' he asked, before spitting juice.

'We're workin' on it, believe me,' Dan answered

him. 'Meantime, we want to hire fresh horses.'

'Leave the sorrel, else take your pick.' Cord winked one of his pale eyes.

They looked over the animals that were in the stalls either side of their own bayo and sabino mounts.

'Looks like a couple o' fleabit greys, then,' Dan said.

'Well, that's all we want. Let's get 'em dressed,' Will replied.

Ten minutes later they were saddled up and leaving the livery.

'Goin' on a picnic?' Cord wondered out loud, and spat more stuff into the ground between his boots.

'Banded Wing. What trail takes us?' Will asked.

'Follow the road west from town. Six miles out, you'll pass close to a turn o' the creek. If your luck's in, you'll see the sign tellin' you you're steppin' on to Banded Wing,' Cord said.

'What's that about *luck?*' Dan asked him.

The livery man had one more long, fearsome dribble, before answering. He showed his brown, Peggy teeth. 'Losin' his herd lost last night's goin' to make Fearon Chappel raise Cain. Yessir, from now on, he'll be givin' orders to shoot people dead. Believe *me.*'

8

THE LINK

As the brothers rode into the street, Rafer Vorn was swinging his own horse away from the hitching rail out front of Beaker's Brim. The owner of the Short Snake was headed towards the western end of the town and the wagon road beyond.

'He's ridin' like there's somethin' burnin',' Dan said. 'I hope it don't turn out to be us.'

'Why should it?' Will replied, when they too continued west beyond the town. 'He don't know where we're headed.'

'Oh no, I didn't think o' that,' Dan called out as he went ahead.

'If all the things you never thought of were bullets, we'd be sellin' to the army,' Will answered to no one in particular.

When they'd nearly ridden the six miles, Will glanced back. There was no one trailing them and the town was hazed as it had been when they'd first rode in.

'I reckon now's when you take a diversion, Dan. Stay to the north, an' within sight. If you hang in close to the creek, there's willow an' stuff for cover. If there's someone out there, you'll see 'em when they move out. Just get 'em before they get me, you hear?'

'Yeah, I hear. But who exactly you thinkin' of?'

'You forgot the warning Cord gave us? We're almost on Chappel's land.'

'OK, Brother,' Dan said. He wheeled his horse and, dramatically low in the saddle, kicked dust in a long, sweeping curve.

Ten minutes on, when the drygulcher fired, Will drew his feet from the stirrups, slid out of the saddle and hit the ground with a thud. He rolled over, kept going until he reached the shelter of a big, lone oak at the side of the dirt road. 'I said to get them before they get *me*,' he yelled drily, spitting dust from his mouth.

A second bullet gouged out grit a few feet from Will's head. 'Get the bastard!' he yelled, while listening to the sound of the gunshot. 'Big fifty, I bet,' he growled. 'Gives him the advantage,' he mused wryly, and hugged the ground.

The fact that the ambusher was using a heavy calibre single-shot rifle was important to Will. It meant that the man would have to reload after each shot. And that could prove to be his undoing.

He knew he was relatively safe, coiled snake-like in the oak roots, waiting for his brother to take a hand. 'Where the hell are you, Dan?' he asked, of the cloudless Nebraska sky.

The rifle roared again, and its sound cracked across the range like a heavy bullwhip. No bullet arrived though, and Will had the sense of the gun's barrel going skyward.

'Dan!' he shouted, and grinned hopefully. He waited, then got to his knees, held his hat against the brightness. He couldn't see the grey, but no more shots came and he wondered about calling for his brother's attention. He didn't, just in case the rifleman was waiting to nail him.

'You comin' in, Will?' he then heard the shout from Dan. 'I got me some kind o' water rat down here.'

Will crouched, made his way forward. Ahead and to his left, was the tangle of creekside vegetation where the rifleman had been hiding out.

But now Dan was standing there, deep in the sedge. With his boot, he'd been pressing the long barrel of a Sharps rifle tight across Lew Deepdish's throat.

'I've never seen him before,' he said. 'You want to ask him about all this?'

'He ain't a total stranger,' Will answered. He leaned down and grabbed at the iron ring the man wore around his neck, pulled him to his knees, for a closer look.

'I know what this is meant to be, accordin' to Cedar Truckle, but this here ain't a shackle link.'

'What's it matter?' Dan asked.

'I'm not sure. Somethin' don't sit right. He is goin' to wake up, ain't he?'

'Yeah, I hardly touched him.'

They both heard the clatter of hoofs through loose stone, and looked quickly towards the sound. Dan lifted the big rifle and Will turned his Colt. Two riders were standing their horses across the shallow bed of the creek. Will relaxed, but not quite enough to lower his gun when he recognized the man.

'Gettin' kinda' busy out here,' Dan remarked, as the riders splashed on through the creek water.

'What's happened?' the young, pale-featured Lester Chappel called out.

'This mule head was out to drygulch me,' Will answered. 'Thought at first it was one o' your men.'

'He's a goddamn Blood Leg,' Chappel blurted. 'That goddamn piece of iron he's wearin's their goddamn badge of office.'

'I'm not so sure, kid. I reckon we're supposed to think that,' Will said, but his interest was almost wholly with the girl.

Sorry, Miss Ivy, he was thinking, as he noticed the Long G brand on the girl's mare.

Chappel saw the look. 'You're a feller with real hunger,' he suggested.

'Yeah, I'm sorry,' Will smiled. 'I know it. Don't mean no disrespect.'

'This is Carly Gordam. Her pa owns the horse ranch,' Chappel said. 'Carly, meet the Glass brothers. Will and Dan.'

Both Will and Dan nodded, tipped their hats. Dan let the Sharps' barrel drop back down, as Deepdish started to move, make groaning noises.

'We'd introduce you, but this here's someone who

don't abide by the niceties o' life,' Will said.

'I'm workin' for Mr Vorn. It was *me* got dry-gulched. Not the way they're tellin' it,' Deepdish lied.

Will shook his head in disbelief and turned to Chappel. 'For the sake of it, let's go with this ring. If it really is a Blood Leg trinket o' some sort, it don't say much for Vorn.'

'Yeah, you're right. There's some answerin' to be done, an' Pa's goin' to enjoy pullin' feathers from this bird.'

'Mine too,' Carly Gordam added, keenly.

Deepdish's jaw dropped. 'Jesus, I was just funnin',' he croaked. 'That was no more'n Lew Deepdish clawin' his way out of a hole.' The man was feeling the sweat crawl over him. He was wondering how much time he'd got left as a hired gun.

Dan pulled him to his feet. 'Shut your squawkin',' he snarled. 'You've done yourself up, an' there's a Vorn smell clingin' to your hide.'

'You need a new nose, mister,' the voice called out from beyond the willows. 'Any o' you makes a move I don't like, an' the girl loses her pretty face.'

A man wearing a cambric hood moved carefully from the trees. He was holding a shotgun that was aimed unswervingly at Carly Gordam.

9

THE CLAMBAKE

'Get movin', Lew,' the man shouted. 'Go straight for your horse. Leave the gun behind. No one's goin' to stop you.'

Deepdish was suddenly aware of another day in the offing. He shrugged insensitively, then pushed at Dan. To show he wasn't hard-pressed, he strutted his way towards the bend in the creek.

But Lester Chappel was less cautious, raring to go. He dug his spurs, knowing that if the masked man fired, he'd collect most of the shot. In an instant, Lester and his high-bred buckskin were in front of Carly Gordam, protecting her from the blast of the shotgun.

'Let's go!' Dan shouted. 'He ain't goin' to get far.'

They headed for the creekside willows. Will to the left, and Dan to the right. But under cover of the dense timber, the man had disappeared.

Dan stood silent, peered intently into the green tangled growth. Will went a little further, before backtracking.

'He's gone,' he said, angrily. 'I thought only the Apache could do that. I guess he was another o' them Blood Legs.'

'Yeah. I did read once that Geronimo's still on the loose,' Will joked. 'That voice was familiar sounding, though,' he said more seriously. Then, 'Look there, Dan.'

Dan shifted his attention to where Will was pointing. He saw a rider who looked like Lew Deepdish. 'There's only one of 'em,' he said.

'Yeah, I know,' Will agreed. 'We still got company.'

But they decided it was foolhardy, perilous to search any further for the masked man. They returned to where Lester and Carly sat their saddles waiting. It wasn't that Lester's courage had deserted him, more that someone had to look out for Carly.

It took Dan ten minutes to retrieve the grey he'd left hidden further out on the grassland. When they all rode from the creek, Lester and Carly were out front. Will was doubled-up on Dan's hired grey.

They were nearing the South Platte wagon road when another group of horsemen appeared from the direction of the town. It was Amos Hatte, and he was flanked by Fearon Chappel and Jasper Stebbs, Chappel's ever-present foreman.

'Can't be anyone left in Wyandot. Now's a good time to rob the bank,' Will muttered.

Dan nodded enthusiastically 'If we weren't havin' a clambake,' he said, and let out a low snigger.

Behind Stebbs rode two other men; one of them leading Will's grey.

'What's been goin' on here, boys?' Hatte enquired. 'We been out to see what trouble's beset some o' the smaller ranches. Caught this Cord bronc about a mile back.'

'You Lobo Creek folk are getting' real tiresome, Sheriff. Why'd you all think it's *us* that knows what's goin' on? I'm beginnin' not to care that much. An' that probably goes for my brother.'

Hatte took a deep breath, looked quickly at Dan, who was nodding. 'Neither do I, truth be told,' he said.

'What's my son doin' with the Gordam kid, I want to know,' Fearon Chappel, snarled out his interuption.

'How's the sheriff supposed to know that, goddamnit?' Lester said defiantly.

It was Carly who spoke up. 'Really, Mr Chappel,' she said, a touch haughtily. 'I thought our families were on friendly terms. Or is it just *me* who's upsetting you?'

'That's my business.' Chappel's nostrils flared above his big, white moustache. 'I don't have to explain to you,' he said.

Dan watched with amused detatchment. Will was thinking, there must be some reason, good or bad, for Chappel to be acting the way he was.

'Yeah, ease off, Fearon,' the sheriff advised. 'People are beginnin' to talk about you an' your ways of late.'

'Does that include you, Amos?' the cantankerous rancher asked.

'To me, it seems an almighty queer time to go upsettin' your neighbours,' Hatte reasoned.

'Maybe I got good reason, *of late*. You considered that?' Chappel's voice was larded with innuendo.

'My God. Pa's got to hear what you're saying,' Carly said, and wheeled her mare away.

'Well done, Pa. Made another goddamn ridiculous accusation,' Lester said, unhappily.

Fearon Chappel's eyes narrowed uncertainly as he watched the girl ride off.

'Let her go, boss,' Jasper Stebbs cut in. 'You said what had to be said.'

'Since when has the hired help told you what to do, eh, Fearon? There's somethin' wrong, ain't there?' the sheriff asked, with some obvious feeling.

Stebbs glared at Hatte, moved his right hand closer to his gun.

The sheriff sucked air noisily between his teeth. 'I might have had my best years, but I'll put you into the ground soon enough,' he snarled threateningly at the Banded Wing foreman.

'Leave it, Jasper!' Chappel barked at his man. 'He means it.'

Dan winked at Will. 'That's what I like about folk out here,' he said cheerfuly. 'It feels like you're among old friends.'

'We got to find out what Chappel thinks is goin' on though,' Will reminded his brother.

Hatte puffed out his cheeks wearily. 'Hand over the horse,' he said to the man holding the reins of Will's grey.

'Pity who meets up with *them* next,' Hatte

muttered, as they sat watching Fearon Chappel ride off, with his son a couple of lengths behind. He looked at Will who was getting back on his own horse. 'How'd you come to lose it anyway?' he asked him.

'I'll tell it like I did to them Chappels,' Will replied. 'Someone callin' himself Lew Deepdish tried to drygulch us . . . well, *me*. My horse got away, and Dan was out on a reconnoitre. We'd been figurin' on somethin' o' the kind. That's about when young Chappel showed with Carly Gordam.' Will attempted a convincing smile for the sheriff. 'Unfortunately, this Deepdish feller ain't with us any more.'

'How come?'

'His guardian angel turned up. Held us under the end of a scatter gun, while he got clean away.'

'Where's *he*, then?'

'If I knew that, I wouldn't be here chewin' the dog with you, Sheriff.'

Hatte consided the gist of Will's story. 'These are my deputies,' he explained, by way of changing tack. 'They rode down from Northport, across the basin. They been lookin' for somethin' might give us a lead on the Blood Legs.'

Will and Dan nodded at the two men.

'You ever heard of this Lew Deepdish?' Will asked them.

The deputies shook their heads.

'He ain't wanted in *these* parts,' Hatte said. 'We best be gettin' back to town. It's wide open at the moment. You comin' with us?' he asked.

Dan was looking at Will and grinning. 'No, we'll stay here,' Will said. 'Miss Ivy'll probably arrive with picnic makin's an' a band, any time now. Maybe we'll see you this evenin'.'

'Conversational bunch,' Dan said of the deputies, as together with the sheriff, they jogged their mounts towards Wyandot. 'Neither of 'em said a word.'

'No. Sheriff weren't too concerned about us not comin' back to town with him,' Will said, thought-fully.

'Should he be?' Dan wondered.

'Yeah, he should. We're takin' point for most o' the trouble that's happened so far.' The brothers rode across the range a mile, then two from the wagon road. Under the shade of another huge oak, they dismounted and ground-hitched the horses. Will unfastened his saddle-bag for his cold luncheon, instead he drew out a much smaller, flat packet.

'What you got there?' Dan asked.

'Not sure. It wasn't here when we left town. I'da noticed.' Will unwrapped the packet, gazed blankly at a wad of crisp bills.

'What the hell's all that?' Dan asked again.

'Can't tell without countin'. Maybe seven hundred dollars,' Will mumbled incredulously. 'There's a piece a paper with somethin' written. It says, er . . . "Boss. We're all ready now. You know, for Wyandot an' Harrison. The Blood Legs are ridin' in an' out. Lew".'

Will thought for no more than a few seconds, then he laughed loudly, 'Jesus, Dan. Do you remember that note I once wrote, to get us both out o' goin' to

61

Sunday School? I signed it, "our mom". Well, this has come from some other catch-penny faker.'

Dan nodded. 'Yeah. What you're sayin' is, if the sheriff found that letter an' the money under your saddle, you'd be branded leader of these Blood Legs. You've been gulled, Brother, an' that means me, too.'

'Yeah, but it's a pretty dumb set-up,' Will agreed. 'It wouldn't last longer'n the next job they pulled. Still, mustn't fret. We just made a year's money the easy way.'

10

THE RIGHTS
AND WRONGS

Deciding their predicament called for some serious thought, Will and Dan sat beneath the broad spread of oak. Will held on to the folding money and his brother looked over the short note.

'What you thinkin' of, Will?' Dan asked, after licking cold bacon grease from his teeth.

'Ahh, this an' that. Who it was shut the door on us. Whether we should ride on, you know. There's a whiff to Oleg Shine an' this Blood Leg business, an' I don't mean the stale sweat of a chain gang.'

'How'd you mean, Dan?'

'It's as if the blame's bein' opportunely shoved back to someone . . . somethin' from the past. There ain't anythin' to hang your hat on, 'cept a doubtful legend.'

'The perpetrators are made up, you mean?'

'Somethin' like that, Dan, yeah.'

'Well, some of it's real enough, Brother.'

Will knew that. 'I know,' he said. 'That's the bit that's keepin' us here. So we don't want anyone findin' all this money about us.'

Will paced off forty feet to a knee-high sapling. He nipped the topshoot, rolled it hard between his fingers. Then he scraped a hole beside the young plant with his clasp-knife, buried the packet of money, and pressed the soil back down with the sole of his boot.

'This marker will be a stunted old oak one day. Let's hope we get back before then,' he said, fittingly subdued.

With a final look around them, they collected their horses and rode back to the wagon road. Quietly waiting for them, Amos Hatte was hunkered on the ground in the shade of his big-bellied roan.

'He's been doin' my thinkin'. I was right all along,' Will rasped quietly to his brother as they got near. 'He's takin' us in.'

The sheriff interpreted the brothers' look. 'I got lucky,' he said agreeably. 'There ain't too many places out here where you can hide from the sun. There was somethin' I shoulda told you earlier. Nestor Midland wants to see you. Both o' you.'

'Was it important enough for you to remember what for, Sheriff?' Dan enquired.

Hatte lifted a pistol style finger and thumb at Dan, smiled an acknowledgement and pulled the make-believe trigger. 'I recall that he didn't rightly say,' he said. 'But when a bank manager says . . . well, you know, boys.'

'No, we don't,' Dan carried on the raillery. 'But there's always stuff to learn.'

The sheriff did a lot of talking on the ride back to Wyandot. He answered questions Will and Dan had about the number and size of ranches in the Lobo Basin and what he thought of the return of Blood Legs.

'Last night's trouble has got me most worried,' Hatte admitted. 'It could be just the start o' big trouble across the basin.'

'A couple o' murders on their own woulda done that,' Dan remarked, coldly.

'So you believe this Oleg Shine has come back? Back from the dead?' Will asked.

'Not if he *was* dead, I don't. Not *dead* certain, anyway,' he said, and smiled. 'I never thought he was behind what these so-called Blood Legs are doin' either.'

'What do you mean? What do you know?' Will asked, getting more interested.

'Shine had somethin' to him. It's difficult to explain. He had his own mind, but I didn't read it as one for more wrong. As if he wanted to make use of a second chance.'

Will felt the twinge of unease again, as they rode into the western end of town. If Amos Hatte was right, he wondered who was alleging the stories of Oleg Shine, of him being a thief and a murderer, and back from the dead, and why. The obvious answer was that it was someone's fanciful, but expedient, decoy.

The trio pulled up in front of the bank as Nestor

Midland came out to welcome them.

'Ahh, glad to see you found them, Amos,' he said, with his usual bombast. 'I was afraid they might have objected.'

The sheriff's two deputies stepped from the bank. Ominously, they moved close behind the sheriff as he dismounted. Will and Dan shared a quick glance, then they too, climbed from their horses, flicked the reins around the hitching rail.

'Why should we object?' Will asked the bank manager. 'The sheriff said you wanted to see us.'

No one spoke for a moment and the doubts hit Will again. He looked at Dan, saw the same thought had occurred to his brother. They were the prime suspects after all, and the trap had been set for them.

'Sorry, boys, I had no other option. I weren't goin' up against both your guns,' Hatte admitted. 'Nestor here says he's got some incriminatin' evidence. Evidence that proves you're with the Blood Legs . . . that you raided the the bank in Harrison. An' there's a brace o' murders that I ain't forgot.' Hatte saw the alarm on Will and Dan's faces. 'But o' course, you ain't under arrest 'til he proves it,' he eased up with.

'That's very true, Sheriff,' Dan said, his body tense, sprung for action.

'Go on, search them,' Midland virtually ordered Hatte. 'My information's that they're carrying monies stole from the Harrison Bank.'

'Signed by our mom,' Will murmured enigmatically, made an inner smile, because he'd divested himself of the dollars.

'If we got more'n three bucks between us, what the

hell makes you think it comes from Harrison?' Dan
bit out the words at Midland.

'They're mixed denomination, fresh printed from
the Philadelphia Mint. I've got their numbers here.
Look them over, Amos,' Midland demanded.

Before the sheriff could make a move, Rafer Vorn
and Cedar Truckle came out of the Beaker's Brim
saloon. The two men looked to see what was happening, crossed the street to the bank.

Dan thrust a hand into a pants pocket, groaned
inaudibly as his fingers touched a crumpled bit of
paper.

Midland saw the anxious look that Dan gave his
brother. 'Go on, search them,' he insisted.

'OK. Take a look through their traps, fellers,' the
sheriff indicated to the deputies.

Promptly, the sworn-in lawmen set to work searching the saddle-bags on the two greys. They found
nothing of interest, and Midland managed to
suppress his raging frustration.

'What you after, Sheriff?' Truckle asked, as he and
Vorn got close. 'Don't look very hospitable.'

'It's Nestor's reliable source. Apparently these two
are the Blood Leg chiefs, an' carryin' a lot o' bills to
prove it. Except that they ain't o' course,' Hatte
explained.

'What dungbrain told you that, Midland?' Truckle
sneered, his animosity towards the banker plain to
see.

'It's confidential. Go through their clothes,'
Midland bellowed with renewed indignation.

'The hell I will, Nestor,' Hatte started off. But he

was immediately outdone by Dan.

'The first one that does that, dies. Lawman or not,' he threatened, his eyes now blazing with intent.

Hatte looked indecisively at Will.

'I'll back him, Sheriff. Those deputies didn't come here to die. We ain't carryin' what Midland's lookin' for. I'll give you what I got.'

Will pulled out the iron ring that he'd taken from Joseph Dace's body. He'd put it in his pocket and almost forgotten it.

'An' *I* got this,' Dan said, holding up the crumpled piece of paper that was ostensibly from Lew Deepdish.

'What's that, Amos?' asked Truckle, seeing the sheriff's concern.

Hatte took the note, read the few words to the assembled group.

Truckle shook his head as he stared at Will and Dan. 'That's a surprise. A let down too.'

'I've just decided I ain't seen you before, mister,' Vorn jeered. 'I ain't been where it would ever be likely.'

Will and Dan didn't say anything. They both felt that words were futile now, even more so, to make a fight of it.

'I'll have to place you both under arrest until I learn the rights an' wrongs o' this. You appreciate that, fellers, don't you?' Hatte said, with jaded irony.

With Hatte and his deputies surrounding them, Will and Dan started off down the street to the jail. By not removing the brothers' guns, the lawmen made it less obvious that the two strangers to

68

Wyandot were being taken into custody. It was the way Hatte wanted it, but it made little difference.

Will glanced back over his shoulder, back towards the bank. He saw Truckle, Midland and Vorn still standing out front. Their eyes met, but Will learned nothing from the mien of their faces.

11

THE TIME TO LEAVE

Along the creek, a frog splashed from the tangled roots of a willow. A hunting fox barked its displeasure, and the sharp sound drifted to the cell window of Wyandot's jail.

'Shut up. At least you're out there,' Will Glass said, ruefully. He sat on the edge of a broken pallet staring at his brother. Until it got too dark to see clearly, Dan had been reading ciphers that had been carved into the stucco'd walls by former occupants.

'Gretchen? That's a girl's name, ain't it?' Dan asked. 'Wonder what she did wrong?'

'It would have been real bad,' Will answered without paying too much attention.

A while later, one of the deputies struck a match,

lit an oil lamp that was hanging in the corridor. It added a low light, but emphasized the intimidating closeness of the cell bars. As expected, he went back to the office without saying a word, banged the door shut behind him.

Will knew they were in danger, that it wouldn't take much for the citizens of Wyandot to organize themselves into a lynch mob. 'They got 'emselves a taste for that sort o' thing,' he reminded them both.

'Hey! Perhaps if we roll our eyes an' make booger men noises, they'll run,' Dan declared. 'They're getting' a taste for that as well, don't forget.'

Will nodded out his agreement and Dan continued, 'I shoulda given you back that message to plant out with the money,' he said.

'Or I should have asked for it,' Will muttered gloomily.

The brothers were in an absorbed hush when the door along the corridor opened again. The same deputy appeared, but now, Cedar Truckle was with him.

'Evenin', boys,' Truckle greeted, as he stepped up to the cell. 'Thought I'd pay you my respects, so to speak. Can I have a private word with these fellers?' he then asked the deputy.

The man shrugged his shoulders, moved off, apparently unconcerned. Will watched him go through the door, back in to the sheriff's office.

'Either he's a trustin' soul, or he's got good reason to leave us alone,' Will observed.

'Amos Hatte trusts me, an' why not? But that's

more'n can be said o' you two. The sheriff ain't convinced about you an' the Blood Legs.'

'What does that mean?' Dan asked.

'It means you should be thinkin o' leavin' here . . . tonight.'

'Why the hurry? The sheriff won't let anythin' happen to us.'

Truckle's forehead crinkled, his eyes squeezed a bit. 'He might not be able to do much about it,' he responded to Will. 'Nestor Midland and Elam Medows are stumpin' up the town as we speak. There's a lot o' folk inclined to believe what they say.' The saloon keeper then pushed a Colt .45 through the bars. 'Take this,' he advised. 'Get out o' here, as soon as you can. If you don't, you'll die for sure.'

'As opposed to *not definite*,' Dan said drily, as Will took the gun.

Truckle quickly put his hands behind his back, as if to remove himself from what was happening. He backed off, turned and walked back to the office, his shadow wavering across the cell walls.

Will glanced at Dan, then sat down heavily on the pallet. They were both wearing their cartridge belts, but the sheriff had relieved them of their guns. Will looked inquisitively at the gun Truckle had given him. He ejected the cartridges from the gun and replaced them with ones from his own belt. Then he placed the Colt beside him on the pallet.

'Now, I'm hungry,' he said. 'Bit of honest, hard work does that to a man. After supper, what say we move out o' this hog hollow, Brother?'

'That'll be somethin' to look forward to,' Dan confirmed.

The door at the end of the corridor opened after they'd patiently waited for a good hour. This time it was Amos Hatte, and he was carrying what was obviously a covered food platter.

'Supper time, means it's my shift,' he said good-humouredly, as he approached the cell door. 'Got this from the May Rooms. They had fried chicken, tonight. Well, that's what Miss Ivy said. Seemed like they was all eatin' plain fixin's to me. Still, here it is. There's coffee in the office.'

The sheriff held the tray in one hand, and unlocked the cell door with the other. Will and Dan stayed sitting calmly on their pallets, Will using his hat to cover the gun.

'Miss Ivy was asking after you both,' Hatte said. 'She wanted to come an' visit, but I told her she'd best wait until tomorrow. She don't believe you two are anythin' to do with the Blood Legs.'

'Not like you then, Sheriff?' Dan ribbed unfunnily. 'Or the bank manager an' his cohort Elam Medows?'

For a moment, Hatte looked uncertain. 'Eat. That's good food,' he said, still thinking on Dan's words.

Five minutes later, Will wiped his face with the cloth that had covered the food. 'That chicken was real fine,' he said, sincerely. 'But you sure it ain't condemned-man's fare, Sheriff?'

'There'll be no more vigilante law from this town,' Hatte asserted from where he stood in the cell doorway. 'This time, I'm holdin' the rope's end.'

Dan got to his feet and looked eagerly along the corridor. 'I think I'll go an' get me that coffee now,' he said intently.

'Yeah, I'll come with you,' Will said, raising himself up.

Smiling uncertainly, Hatte took a step back. 'What're you boys on about? Go on, get back in there,' he said.

'No, you sit down, Sheriff. We got to leave, anyway.' Will drew the Colt from behind his back. He pushed the barrel gently against Hatte's fleshy jawline. 'This ain't a magical ruse,' he advised.

Dan stepped forward and lifted the sheriff's .45 out of its holster. He tried the balance and nodded his appreciation. 'Nice piece,' he said. 'I'll look after it.'

'You're makin' a mistake, boys,' Hatte said quietly.

Will removed the keys from where they were tucked into the sheriff's belt. 'I think I know what you mean,' he said. 'It ain't how Cedar Truckle figures it though. An' don't make a fuss. If you do, them that want to string us up just might vent their disappointment on *you*. So keep quiet.'

Dan chuckled at Will's threat and locked the cell door. They left Hatte sitting disconsolately, used a second key to unlock the narrow rear door of the jail. Will drew back the upper and lower bolts. A cool breeze swept in, and he looked out into the deep darkness. Clouds rolled across the yellowy moon, and there was the smell of approaching rain.

'Careful, Will,' Dan whispered urgently. 'There's somethin' about this I don't like.'

'Yeah, tell me somethin' I don't know, Brother. But we got to keep goin' now,' Will replied as he moved into the night.

12

THE ROAD TO BANDED WING

Dan was close behind Will when they cleared the jail. They'd lost the cover of the small building, and it was almost immediately that a blast of gunfire exploded from the shadows. Will felt as though a gobbet of skin was being chewed from his left arm, knew he'd narrowly missed a more lethal bullet.

His mind's eye retained the after image of the gun's flash, but his peripheral vision made out the blackness of a moving figure. In an instant he fired off two shots. Dan was doing the same, shooting full on, at where the the attacker was reckoned to be.

There was no mistaking the pained suppressed grunt, the sound of a heavy man falling hard to the ground. Dan and Will were hunkered down, their Colts covering open ground ahead of them. In the darkness, a man lay sprawled and lifeless, another took flight, his boots pounding the hard-packed dirt.

'I doubt they'da tried that if they'd known how good we were,' Dan rasped in the ensuing silence. 'How many d'you reckon, Will? Half a dozen?'

'Two. We should have been easy meat.'

'Well, that learned 'em. Only old boots are easy,' Dan jeered.

Will reloaded his gun, glanced back as the rear door of the jail banged open. Against the weak light from inside, the silhouetted shapes of two men loomed.

'Now it's the goddamn deputies. Let's get out o' here,' Dan recommended.

The brothers ran from one dark blocky shape to another. Closer into the town, they hung in to the deep cover afforded by unlit, shadowed buildings.

'Let's get to the livery stable,' Will said. 'Now's when we really do have to clear this town.'

'Why don't you just gather me up, Brother. I can hardly breathe.'

'We'll walk then. Slow and cautious.'

Further along the yards and outbuildings of the main street, a wedge of pale light fell through a half-open gate at the rear of the livery stable.

Will went through first, the palm of his hand in contact with the butt of his holstered Colt. He took cautiously, quiet steps, blinked at the lantern that was hanging from a nail under the hay mow.

Richmond Cord stepped from the near end of the stalls. 'Sounds to me like you found that trouble after all,' he said, his walnut-stocked shotgun wavering between Will and Dan.

'It found *us*,' Dan answered him. 'There's some bobtails changed their minds about wantin' us out o' jail,' he said. 'An' bushwhackin's a specialism o' the Lobo Basin.'

Cord nodded as if he understood, moved the twin barrels off target. 'Is that so?' he rasped. 'Some folk do the strangest things. One o' them Northport deputies brought my horses back,' he added casually. 'You owe me four dollars even for the hire of 'em.'

Without taking his eyes off Cord, Will moved his hand away from his Colt, reached into a pocket of his pants. He drew out money that Amos Hatte had returned to him, handed over four bills to the stable owner.

Cord lowered his shotgun, leaned it against the wall. 'Come to think of it, the cell o' that jail ain't much of a place to stay,' he said. 'I was put in there once for bein' drunk an' disorderly somewhere I shouldn'ta been.'

'Where was that, then?' Dan asked.

'The jail. I was playin' checkers with the sheriff.'

As the men's cagey laughter faded, Will and Dan heard the distinctive click of a gun hammer being cocked.

On impulse, Will spun on his heel to face the door, his right hand already drawing his Colt. He threw himself to one side as he fired, the sound of his gun and that of the assailant melding as one booming blast. A bullet whistled by his head, thudded into a cross beam beside the oil lamp.

Dan swore, waved Richmond Cord away from the line of fire. Will made another, more exacting shot through the doorway, held his fire and looked to his brother, then Cord, who was reaching for his shot-gun.

A man took one pace forward, held up, then took another. He staggered his way through the door. He wore a plain trail outfit, had an iron ring that clinched his neck cloth.

'Deepdish,' exclaimed Dan. 'Thought you'd be swimmin' the Platte, by now.'

Will pushed himself upright, stood silently watching the man who'd earlier tried to shoot him down. His gun felt heavy, and he let it fall into his hoster. He was suddenly worn down, as he saw that the man called Deepdish was fatally wounded.

Deepdish was cursing weakly, using the same cuss words over and over again, as he slumped into a pile of fat grain sacks. He groaned, twisted his head to one side, and a revolver fell from his limp fingers. 'I had to come back,' he grated. 'Don't like to leave a job unfinished. Besides, I was only given a day or so.'

'A day or so, for what?' Will demanded to know. 'Who're you speakin' of?' Will was now bending over Deepdish's bleeding body. 'Is this somethin' to do with Blood Legs?'

'Yeah. The boss ordered me to do it. He ain't long on requests.'

'Well, this time he ain't comin' to your aid,' Will said harshly. 'You're talkin' o' Rafer Vorn, ain't you?'

'You got a guardian angel ridin' with you, Glass,' the gunman, scarcely managed. 'The man you're talkin' about's. . . .' But Lew Deepdish didn't say any more. His eyes opened and flickered and closed, then he rolled sideways into the floor. 'This ain't a good endin',' he garbled, before dying.

Cord stepped across the floor of the livery to pick up his shotgun. 'I guess I shouldn'ta put it down,' he reasoned mysteriously, his eyes moving from Dan to Will.

The brothers collected up their gear, saddled their own sabino and bayo mares. Richmond Cord stood guarding the back door as they readied to leave.

'Keep your powder dry,' Dan advised him. 'Whoever comes through that door first ain't goin' to be blowin' kisses.'

'Ain't that the truth,' Cord muttered, watched inscrutably as Dan and Will spurred into the darkness.

13

THE PAYING BACK

They were nearly two miles outside of Wyandot when Dan pulled up beside his brother. 'Where we goin', Will?' he asked him.

'The place we been meanin' to get to.'

'Yeah, that's what I thought. Why don't we rest up a minute? You can put somethin' around that wound o' yours.'

'It don't hurt none. No worse'n a horse bite,' Will answered, and spurred his sabino back into a lope.

A few miles beyond where they'd run into Lew Deepdish's Big Fifty rifle, the heavy bough of an old oak held a sign for the Banded Wing ranch.

'So far so good,' Dan said, warily.

The men noticed the willow that clumped along the creek to one side of the oak: it was dark and forbidding and, once again, Will felt the apprehen-

81

sion, the shivery grind across his skin. He walked the
mare forward, his hand sweatily gripping the butt of
his Colt.

As Will and Dan pulled their mounts around the
gloomy shadow of trees, two armed men stepped out.

'Where're you two *hombres* goin'?' one of them
demanded to know.

'If this is Banded Wing land, we're already here,'
Will replied, smartly. 'We come to see Fearon
Chappel.'

'Late, ain't it? The boss ain't seein' visitors, even
daytime,' the lookout growled.

'Things don't always work out the way you want
'em. Chappel knows that, an' he'll see us,' Will said,
firmly.

'What's your business?' the man asked. His
companion, at ease, stared hostilely.

'That's with Chappel,' Will told him abruptly.

'I'll get the horses, Ben,' the surly man said. 'Two
of 'em ain't goin' to cause too much trouble.' He
stepped back into the trees, reappeared almost
immediately leading two horses by the reins. The
lookouts pushed their rifles into the saddle boots
and mounted, indicated for Dan and Will to ride
ahead.

For another three miles, the four men rode in
silence. Then the lights from a sprawl of buildings
flickered through the night.

'Jeez. Looks like a small town,' Dan said in
surprise.

They rode forward to one of two hitching rails that
flanked the front terrace of the immense ranch

house. The lookout who'd first challenged them, swung from his horse and looped his reins. Will and Dan reined in their own mares, while the other man sat his saddle and watched anxiously.

'Wait here,' Ben said. 'I'll see if the boss'll see you. You didn't tell us your names.'

'Tell him it's the Glass brothers,' Dan told him.

Will was growing restless, Dan even more so, when Ben came back two minutes later.

'Bill,' he called to his partner. 'We're to bring 'em in. It's OK.'

The man named Bill dismounted, followed Will and Dan up the broad steps as the rain splattered against the deep overhang.

They went through an iron-strapped door, found themselves in a well-lighted, two-storey high hallway. There were many doors off, and patterned cow hides lay across the gleaming waxed floor. Directly ahead, a staircase curved its way to a mezzanine and upper rooms. Ben stopped before a door to the right and knocked.

From behind the panelled door they heard Chappel's voice. Will and Dan looked at each other and grinned foolishly. Ben opened the door and motioned them into a step-down room with big furniture. Fearon Chappel sat in a leather upholstered wing-back. He was holding a cigar, looking confidently up at them.

'Good evenin', gentlemen,' he said. 'Ben tells me you have important business. It must be, to risk your lives.'

'We weren't riskin' anythin' an' you know it, Mr

83

Chappel,' Will said. 'We look at it more like them riskin' theirs.'

'Very good.' Chappel acknowledged Will's confidence. 'All right, boys,' he then told Bill and Ben. 'You can return to the creek gap.'

Chappel waited a moment for the men to close the door behind them. 'Well, we're alone now. What is it brings you here?'

Will got the nod from his brother to proceed. 'We just escaped from the Wyandot jail,' he said calmly. 'We were arrested and accused o' bein' leaders of the Blood Legs.'

'You rode out here to tell me that?' Chappel enquired, looking from Dan to Will.

'Not quite. The Blood Legs raided Harrison an' Wyandot, but it was your *cattle* they stole. So, while my brother was studyin' cave paintin', I got to wonderin' why you ranchers are doin' diddly squat about it. You're shiverin' in your boots 'cause you think a dead man's come back to life. If you an' the rest of the ranchers around here had any sense you'd round up your outfits and drive that bunch o' murderin' renegades, or *whoever* they are, right out o' Lobo Basin.'

'Hmm, I, too, been wonderin' about that. But what makes you so interested in what we're doin' about it?' Chappel asked.

Will's eyes narowed. 'Let me tell you a story,' he said, with more intensity.

Will then told about what had happened to him and Dan since they'd arrived the previous morning. How they'd found the body of Joseph Dace in Ivy

May's hotel, about the door being pushed to, and the attempt of Lew Deepdish to bushwhack them. Dan spoke of the money, and the letter that Will had found hidden in his saddle-bags.

Will explained how Cedar Truckle had given them a gun to help them escape from the jail. Of the men who'd tried to shoot them down as they did so. Then, Deepdish's final, doomed attempt to kill them inside the livery stable.

'So, Mr Chappel, if *that* ain't an arrangement to get us interested, I'd like to know what the hell is,' Will concluded, to Chappel's stony face.

'You put it like that, an' it does look like someone's mighty anxious to get your blood spilled,' Chappel conceded. 'It's beginnin' to look like Blood Legs ridin' through the basin's a tad more than Oleg Shine jumpin' from his grave.'

'Yeah, I been thinkin' that, all along,' Will said. 'There's got to be an explanation for what's been happenin'. For instance, I heard someone talkin' o' the Union Pacific layin' down a spur from Julesburg.'

'Well, maybe these goddamn Blood Legs heard it too,' Dan contributed. 'They could be tryin' to mop up the ranchers ahead o' time. Some sort o' railroad sooners.'

'It's a notion,' Chappel said. 'An' with Joe Dace already dead, that leaves three big ranches between the Platte rivers. Nitch Gordam, Rafer Vorn, an' me. If we were to join old Joe, I reckon someone could buy up most o' the basin, an' pretty cheap too. Lester's my only kin, and the same with Gordam an' his daughter. I don't know if Vorn has any relatives. I know there's none that's close.'

'Yeah. An' he probably sees us as trouble. . . . So you see, Mr Chappel, we got to do some fast talkin' . . . get ourselves a contingent for stayin' alive. You owe me that.'

'Yes, I seem to remember. What else you got on your mind?'

'A couple o' things. Why is it that a man as powerful as you's got a sidewinder like Cedar Truckle movin' him around?'

'Well, if that's what he's doin', it'll be for me to know, and for me to deal with. Not you.'

'Fair enough,' Will accepted doubtfully.

Chappel inspected the end of his cigar. 'So what's the other thing?' he asked.

Will tried a smile. 'Why you're givin' your kid an' Carly Gordam such a hard time?'

'You enjoy journeyin' to where the trouble is, don't you, Glass?' Chappel suggested, his colour rising.

'Before time gets to me,' Will countered. 'Hell, it weren't so long ago, I was their age. An' you musta been young once. Like a lot o' things round here, it seems irrational . . . mighty unreasonable. I'm thinkin' maybe there's some connection.'

'There ain't no connection. The trouble's between me an' Nitch Gordam. If the kids have to suffer, so be it, an' that's all I'm sayin' on the matter. Now it's late, so I'll be thankin' you—'

Chappel was mid-sentence when a rear window

shattered with a crash. The bullet thumped past Dan and embedded itself in the timber-panelled wall.

Chappel swore, immediately blew out the reading lantern on the table beside him. Will doused a wall sconce and Dan did the same for the hanging lamp. The cavernous room was then plunged into darkness, as the tall, narrow window in the front corner of the building exploded.

'That ain't the neighbourly way to say good evenin',' Dan said, his voice scratchy. 'They got us surrounded.'

'Blood Legs have arrived. I wondered how long,' Chappel muttered.

Will remembered the layout of the room; in the deep dark, made it to the nearest window. He couldn't see much in the weak light from the ranch's outbuildings, but a volley of gunfire suggested the bunkhouse was also being hit.

'How many men you got out there?' Will asked.

'There's a dozen, all in,' Chappel said. 'But some of 'em will have gone into town.' The ranch owner was now standing alongside the other wrecked window. 'If Oleg Shine ain't dead, if he is leadin' them Blood Legs, I know why he's come right in here.'

'Why?' Dan asked, kicking out at shards of glass across the floor.

'I was one o' them who strung him up,' Chappel confessed, in the fearfully charged atmosphere.

14

THE ATTACKERS

'You thinkin' what *I'm* thinkin,' Dan called out to his brother, as more gunshot peppered the house.

'Probably,' Will answered. 'Fryin' pans an' fires comes to mind. I reckon this time we're in real trouble, bein' stuck here.'

'A rifled cannon couldn't break through these timbers,' Chappel railed.

'That's true. But if it *is* Oleg Shine, he'll *burn* this place down around us. An' from what you say, who's to blame him?' Dan countered.

'Why the hell didn't your two lookouts do somethin' about it?' Will added to the reproaches. 'They coulda fired a warnin' shot.'

'They rode east. This murderous bunch woulda come in from the McConoughy lake. That's to the west o' here.'

'How do we know it ain't Amos Hatte and his

deputies?' Dan asked, as he edged to the corner window.

'They wouldn't be shootin up the place, for God's sake,' Chappel snapped.

'Yeah. I reckon Shine's desire to gut Mr Chappel, is more'n Hatte wantin' us back in his rotten jail,' Will said.

Dan grunted, pushed his Colt through the shattered window beside Chappel, let off two shots into the darkness.

'What guns have you got here?' Will asked Chappel.

'There's rifles in the rack, an' I got an army revolver in the drawer.'

'Well, all we've got is our belt cartridges. So we're goin' to need them rifles if they decide to make a night of it,' Will said. He was still peering from the side of the window, when he glimpsed someone in a gleaming wet slicker. He took a fast shot and swore. 'Your boys that's holed up in the bunkhouse can at least keep 'em busy,' he suggested to Chappel. 'At least stop 'em from comin' through the front door.'

The rain had eased and the sky had lightened, and Dan moved a shutter across the open window. He watched, blinked, stared for another moment, until he was sure. Against the skyline he saw riders advancing from the far side of the home ground.

'Riders comin',' he said. 'There's a few of 'em, an' if they're support for this bunch, we really ought to get goin', Brother,' he said grimly.

Across the ranch-house yard, the roaring of the guns suddenly grew more intense. 'Come an' see this,' Dan called out to Will. 'These fellers have got their own little war goin' on.'

Chappel stood back, and Will elbowed the shutter, took a slanting look out front of the house.

'The enemy of the enemy,' he murmured. 'They're our dearest friends, whoever they are,' he said a bit louder.

For five minutes it sounded like the fighting stormed around the out-buildings, and on all sides of the house.

'This is how Davy Crockett musta felt,' Dan yelled.

'They killed him,' Chappel pointed out, 'an' reduced the Alamo to a pile o' rubble.'

The three men faced into the room with their backs against the wall. They daren't move around or risk any more shooting from the windows. They couldn't break up the factions that were fighting, for fear of hitting an ally.

Then, abruptly, the attackers suspected of being the Blood Leg gang, withdrew. They split up, ran for the deep shadows of the barns and sheds, then for their horses they'd tied in back among the surrounding timber. The new arrivals were on their heels though, poured lead across the range in their send off.

Will could now see there was a handful of men who'd come to the timely aid of the Banded Wing outfit. 'Whoever they are, they're well met,' he said.

'Hey, Pa, you in there?' the strong, youthful voice of Lester Chappel then hollered. 'We come to help.'

'It don't ever come too late,' Dan muttered, wryly.

'Who's that you got with you?' was Chappel's yelled response.

'Mr Gordam. He's brought his men.'

'Gordam!' Chappel blustered. 'What in hell's name does he want?'

'A bear hug might be in order,' Dan suggested, with more sarcasm.

Lester Chappel had drawn in close to the front terrace. He was astride his thoroughbred buckskin, held up a Winchester rifle. 'You can put your heads up an' come out now. We got control,' he confirmed.

From inside the house, a match flickered then glowed as Chappel moved back to the table lamp. As the light spread, the three men looked around them. Glass was strewn across the floor and the wall panelling was splintered and holed from the attackers' bullets. There was one hole in the wing-back, just above and to one side of where Chappel's head had been less than ten minutes earlier.

'Is that good fortune or what?' Will mused, as he and Dan sided Chappel to the front of the house.

In the lighted hallway, the three men stopped. Will and Dan levelled their Colts, watched tensely as Lester pushed the door open and inwards with the barrel of his rifle.

'Couldn't be too sure you weren't in there with a gun to your head,' the young Chappel said, with an uncertain smile. The men behind him stood hesitantly on the terrace steps.

'It's your home, boy. Come on in,' his father said. 'That's all o' you,' he added, with some difficulty.

'I ain't been welcome here for a while, Fearon,' an

ageing man with a deeply lined face, rasped.

'You ain't snatched me from the jaws o' death for a while, you old goat.' Chappel turned his big, hawk nose at Nitch Gordam.

Gordam pulled his well-worn hat from his head, stepped forward stiffly. 'Don't expect me to paddle paws. That sort o' stuff'll take longer,' he grumbled.

'Just come in,' Chappel sniffed, wiped the back of his hand across his heavy white moustache.

Chappel crossed the hallway with Gordam, Lester and one of the Long G waddies. Will and Dan held their ground when Jasper Stebbs suddenly appeared through a doorway beside the staircase. The Banded Wing foreman was grimly eyeing the men who were entering Chappel's living-room.

It was the same thought that instantly occurred to Dan and Will. Where had Stebbs been during the raid?

'Been hidin', or just sleepin' sound?' Dan asked, his voice heavy with scorn.

'Get out,' Stebbs snarled. 'I don't want you anywhere near this ranch.'

'So all of a sudden there's a new boss?' Dan retaliated.

'Get out, an' stay away from Banded Wing land,' Stebbs went on.

'Jasper!' Fearon Chappel shouted from across the hallway. 'I give the orders inside my own house. You know somethin' about these men I don't?'

'It's the stench o' the can. They brought it in with 'em, Mr Chappel.'

Very quickly, Will fired the question. 'When were

you in town, Stebbs?'

Stebbs's lip curled. 'I ain't been in town. Not since seein' you there. Why?'

'Well, how else would you know where we been? Unless, o' course, you been listenin' at doors.'

'I don't like the sound o' that, Jasper.' Chappel glared angrily at his foreman. 'That sort o' thing shouldn't happen under my roof. You been skulkin' inside while we're all bein' cut to pieces. Pack your traps. Be gone by midday tomorrow.'

'Oh yeah? Well, I'll just go an' see if there's any work with Amos Hatte. Do that, shall I, Mr Chappel?' the foreman asked deviously. 'When the deputies move on, he'll be wantin' someone to talk to.'

'Get yourself to the bunkhouse,' Chappel demurred. 'We'll talk of this later.'

'An' what about these two scouts?' Stebbs persisted.

Chappel bit his lip, flexed the fingers of his hands. 'Maybe it would be for the best if you rode away now,' he said, his eyes flitting uneasily between Dan and Will. 'The sheriff might stump up some abettin' charge, if he finds out you're here.'

The brothers glared disappointedly at Chappel, defiantly at Stebbs, then moved out on to the wide puncheon terrace, slowly took the steps to the yard.

Dan pulled his slicker from behind his saddle. 'I don't understand,' he said. 'Chappel ain't the kind o' man who scares easy. But he was . . . is.'

'Yeah. Stebbs is holdin' a pressure card. It's somethin' Chappel don't want the sheriff to know about. It'd be interestin' to know what that card is.'

'Why don't we go right back in an' ask?'

'Yeah. Be good, wouldn't it? But it's back to Wyandot. We should be lookin' for the goddamn leaders of these Blood Legs.'

As the rain drifted away, the sky cleared and the moon glowed from out of the dark clouds.

'What's on your mind?' Dan asked, after ten minutes' riding.

'I was thinkin' that young Chappel brought Gordam and his best men tonight. The Blood Legs woulda got clean away, even though they got the Long G waddies chasin' 'em. But even so . . .'

'Yeah, and. . . ?' Dan was eager to know.

'You remember me sayin' when woulda been a good time to rob the Wyandot bank?' Dan asked.

'When everyone was out o' town.' Dan cottoned-on immediately. 'Got it,' he said eagerly. 'You reckon they'll be runnin' for Nitch Gordam's place.'

'That's it, Brother. You figure we should pay 'em a visit?'

'Hell no. We coulda met the old reaper by helpin' one o' these big-shot ranchers. An' that was up against someone who's at least got a claim on retribution. Chappel showed his gratitude by kickin' our asses. I'd say we done our share o' good deedin', Will.'

Will took off his hat, beat it a couple of times against his leg before replacing it.

'Yeah, I knew you'd think that,' he said, 'but it wouldn't do any harm to look the place over. Sheriff told us the spread's about four miles south o' the wagon road, didn't he?'

94

'Yeah. An' I shoulda guessed you'd sucker me with another scrap.' Dan laughed into the night. 'But Carly Gordam's features do have the beatin' of Amos Hatte's sweaty old chops, I suppose.'

15

THE TALL TALE

Will took out his stemwinder and read the time by the light of a match.

'What's it say?' Dan asked.

'A minute off eleven,' Will said, and tucked the watch back into a pocket.

They lapsed into a long silence as they rode on, each with their own thoughts on how they'd handle the situation ahead.

Eventually, they topped a low rise, stopped among the sharp, rising scent of clover. Nestling at bottom of the incline, they could make out the forbidding shadows of stables, breaking pounds and feed sheds.

'That's got to be the Long G,' Dan said. 'It's a horse breeding set-up. But it sure don't look as though there's much goin' on.'

'We're meant to think that,' Will said, after considering the layout. No lights shone from the ranch house or its outbuildings and he didn't like it. 'There's someone there. An' not just those who should be.'

They rode quietly across the hard-pummelled ground that fronted the ranch house. The front door was a gaping hole of blackness in the shadows beneath the overhang. Will and Dan slid from their saddles, let the reins of their horses drop to the ground.

'Let's go take a look,' Will said softly. 'I've got a bad feelin' about this.'

They walked carefully up the steps, stopped to listen at a front window near to the open doorway. The window had a shade almost fully drawn, allowed a sliver of light to run across the sill. They just picked out the murmur of voices within, when from one of the buildings at the side of the house, a horse nickered, stirred restlessly. They drew their Colts and edged their way through the doorway. From the left, they heard the voices again, though couldn't make out any words. Will pushed his left hand out and ran it along the wall, advanced towards more light that crept from beneath the ranch-house's closed parlour door.

Dan shuffled along, until they both heard the voices more clearly. It was Rafer Vorn who took up the conversation.

'Tell me another reason for him comin' in here,' he said. 'It had to be a ruse. A trick to get your pa out to Banded Wing.'

'No. The Lester I know wouldn't do that,' Carly

Gordam objected. 'You think I wouldn't know if he was capable of that?'

'I wouldn't like to say, miss. But you got to remember he's a Chappel, but not strong enough to defy his old man.'

'But why would he do such a thing?' Carly persisted.

'It was the Chappel way to end a grievance with your pa, once an' for all. Soon as I heard, I rode straight here. I'm so sorry, Miss Carly.'

'What happened, Mr Vorn?' Carly asked with dawning alarm.

'The Blood Legs. They were waiting there. I don't reckon any o' them had much of a chance.'

'If you're telling me my father is dead, I don't believe you. I won't believe you,' Carly said shakily.

'That's what it was all about, Carly,' Vorn continued with his line. 'It looks like your pa knew too much.'

'Knew too much about what? And what're these hellish Blood Legs to do with it? What *are* you talking about?' Carly asked, the bleakness starting to fade her voice.

'Can't you guess, Miss Carly? Who'd you think *were* the Blood Legs?' Vorn asked with the offensive overtone.

'Jeez, he don't mess about with a story, does he?' Dan said, almost choking on his words. 'The girl's set to believe him.'

'No, she's not,' Will said, and kicked open the door. He stood threateningly in the opening,

98

covered Vorn with his Colt. 'What's this? The fairy-tale as told by Vorn?' he asked, icily.

Vorn was less than ten feet away, sitting opposite Carly Gordam. 'What the—? You two are—' he spluttered in shock, grabbed at the arms of the chair.

'Your pa's all right, Carly,' Will said. 'Lester took him an' some o' your men over to the Banded Wing. They arrived in time to drive off the Blood Legs. We know that, 'cause we just rode from there.'

'Of course you did,' Vorn, butted in sharply. 'I was in town when Hatte arrested you. He had you thrown in jail on suspicion o' bein' their leaders. Where else but Chappel's protection would you run to, when you broke out?'

'Oh right, that explains it,' Dan said, with mock flippancy.

Carly looked from Dan to Will. 'So my pa isn't dead, Mr Glass?' she asked, shocked and bemused.

'He couldn't be more alive. In fact, when we last saw him, he was bein' invited into Chappel's den for some lost-time roosterin'.'

'That's right kiddo,' Dan added gladly. 'We heard 'em bury their differences, whatever they were. Now, if you wouldn't mind turnin' away, me an' Mister Vorn need to get somethin' sorted out.'

With that, Dan stepped forward and relieved Vorn of the revolver he carried beneath his coat. 'Don't want you fightin' back,' he said, uncaringly.

'What the hell you goin' to do?' Vorn asked, nervously.

Dan punched the man hard and high in the side of his head. 'How many more times do I have to do this?' he snapped, thinking back to what happened in the Ivy May rooms.

Will swallowed hard and shook his head, shrugged hopelessly as he locked eyes with Carly.

'Now, you tell Miss Carly here, that you just lied,' Dan rasped impatiently at Vorn. 'You tell her that her young suitor's as worthy as she says.'

Vorn held a hand up to the side of his face, worked his jaw. 'Yeah,' he groaned, 'your pa's OK . . . as far as I know.'

'That's better,' Dan told him. 'I'm beginnin' to hurt from crackin' the bones o' your skull.'

Will moved in and dragged Vorn to his feet, roughly pushed him towards the door. 'I don't know who you're workin' with, mister,' he said, 'but I'd think real serious about your next move. From now on, you ain't got too many left.'

'I'm guessin' that's your mount we heard earlier. Get it an' ride,' Dan said, with resounding menace. 'If we ever meet again, I'll return that revolver. Then I'll show you what scarin' someone really means.'

When Dan and Will went back into the house, they found that Carly had lighted some more lamps, another one in the parlour. She smiled with tearful relief as they came into the room.

'He's gone?' she asked tiredly.

'Yeah, he's gone,' Will confirmed. 'What I want to know is, what was he after? Why was he spinnin' you such a yarn?'

'I know part of it,' Carly said. 'When he came into the house and called out, I was in my own room. I wasn't asleep because I was worried about Pa and Lester. He said that I ought to get dressed up for a ride, that Pa was badly wounded and wanted to see me. He said he'd take me there.'

'Yeah, I bet he would,' Dan sneered.

'When he realized I didn't believe him, he changed the story. He said Lester was leading Pa and our boys into a trap.'

'Yeah, we heard that bit. Sounds like he wanted to get you away from the ranch,' Will said.

'I know,' Carly nodded slowly. She was still puzzled, still worried.

'I can hear riders,' Dan called out. 'If it's the chain gang from Lake McConoughy, I'm goin' to shoot me some this time. Let's get ready for 'em.'

Clutching Vorn's revolver, Carly got herself safely shut away in the scullery at the rear of the house. Dan and Will turned down the parlour lamps and sat in the darkness, waiting.

After an interminable five minute's, there was footsteps on the porch, then in the hall. When Nitch Gordam appeared in the doorway he was lighted by the weak light from the hallway lamp. Will flicked a match and Dan murmured a quiet, relieved oath.

Looking into the barrels of two Colts, Gordam was momentarily surprised. But he wasn't a man to scare easy, and didn't even lift his rifle. 'What the hell you boys doin' here?' he asked. 'Not that you ain't welcome.'

'We'll get your kid. She can tell you,' Dan said, good-humouredly. 'Me an' Will still got a meetin' planned with the Sheriff o' Wyandot.'

'That's right,' Will agreed, and holstered his Colt. 'We really have to go for these Blood Legs now some folk are acceptin' they ain't us.'

16

THE BROKEN CHAIN

Will and Dan rode into Wyandot, into the near deserted back end of the town and stopped in front of the livery stable.

Will dismounted. He handed the sabino's reins to Dan, went to the closed door of the stable and knocked. There was no answer, and he knocked louder. A full minute later, the door opened and Richmond Cord stood there fully dressed.

His jaw dropped as he looked at Will, then beyond to Dan. 'I'm havin' me a nightmare,' he muttered. 'You two must think you can cheat the Devil.'

'We're still tryin', old feller,' Dan said, touching the brim of his hat.

'Can you take our horses in for the night, or what's left of it?' Will asked. 'We're goin' back to Ivy's Rooms.'

'That's what you did last time,' Cord said wryly.

'Yeah, but times change,' Dan grinned, as he climbed down from his bayo.

'Open up,' Will said.

Cord stepped back inside, drew the bolts from the rest of the big door. Immediately, Will saw that the body of Lew Deepdish was gone.

'You were one o' the men who attended Oleg Shine's hangin', weren't you, Mr Cord' he said.

'You askin' or tellin'?' Cord answered, slow and foxy like.

'Tellin'. Who else was there?' Will's voice was turning hard and emotionless.

'There was seven of us: Cedar Truckle, Joe Dace an' Garnet' Coddle, the Chappels, an' Benton May an' me. I didn't like the idea of a lynchin' though. I didn't stay . . . didn't see when they strung him up.'

'There's always someone that don't know what they do, eh, Will?' Dan called, as he led the horses in. His disgust for Cord's absolution was quite clear.

'So, what did you do with Deepdish's body after we left?' was Will's next question.

'Got someone to remove it, o' course. This place smells bad enough as it is.'

Will agreed, didn't want to stay around any longer. 'We'll be goin',' he said.

Cord slammed the door shut after the brothers had walked from the stable. From just outside they heard the bolt sliding back into place. The chair in which Cord usually sat out front of the building, was propped against the wall.

'Hey, remember Cedar Truckle sayin' that *all* your enemies ain't ever dead?'

'Yeah, I remember,' Dan said. 'You think he had us in mind?'

'Let's go an' find out. Ask some goddamn questions.'

Warily, the two men kept close to the town buildings' shadows. Halfway along the street, they turned into an alley that sided the Beaker's Brim saloon.

'I hope he's here,' Dan said, nodding at a door that had a window alongside it.

Will raised himself on his toes and looked in. 'Yeah,' he murmured. 'I can see him at his desk. Must be his office. Hey Truckle,' he then called out. 'Let us in. It's Will an' Dan Glass. We want to talk to you.'

Cedar Truckle's head came up quickly. His watchful eyes met Will's through the window, and he made a move to unlock the door.

Inside the office, Dan quickly locked the door and pulled down the window blind. Truckle turned back to his chair and sat down heavily.

'I thought you'd be long gone by now,' he said, casting an eye on his Winchester above the door lintel. 'But who knows what you two'll do next.'

'Yeah. We're as unpredictable as you, Truckle,' Dan said drily.

'Where'd you get the .45 you gave me?' Will asked.

'From right here. There's always one or two. You come by 'em in a job like mine. Why? Does it matter?'

'I'm just wonderin'.'

'I picked it up an' brought it to the jail. It was fully loaded wasn't it?'

Dan and Will exchanged a questioning glance. 'Yeah, it was fully loaded. I exchanged the cartridges though. Just to make sure,' Will said.

'What're you suggestin'?' Truckle looked at him in astonishment. 'You thought I had you set up, for when you broke jail? The final surprise?'

The brothers looked at each other again. 'Well, yeah,' Will offered less brashly. 'Whether you knew about it or not.'

'You managed to shoot that feller outside o' the jail. The deputies found him within minutes.'

'Yeah, but there's one or two got away.'

'So, why'd you not put a bullet in me right off, instead o' comin' here near friendly?' Truckle insisted.

'Because there's a doubt.'

'What doubt? I reckon I'd be better off knowin'.'

'The Beaker's Brim's the only saloon in town, an' it does good business, right?'

'Well, I got no debts.'

'Exactly. Only a beef-wit would risk that by runnin' around stealin' cattle, an' robbin' himself. An' you get to kill enough people from right outside o' here. Why be unlawful? No, Truckle, I don't reckon you're a captain o' the Blood Leg Guard,' Will reasoned.

The three men were considering their situations when, in the short, ensuing silence, there was a sharp rap on the alley door. They glanced at each other and Dan trembled once again with curious unease.

Truckle hauled himself up and went to the door.

He hesitated and looked back at the brothers.

'Better you weren't here,' he whispered. 'Get in the stores room until I find out who it is.'

Will and Dan moved in among the consumables for the saloon and pushed the door, most of the way shut.

Truckle unlocked and opened the door to the alley, stepped back when he was confronted by a tall, spare-framed man who loomed there in the semi-darkness.

The man's grey eyes bored deep into Truckle's startled, nonplussed face. 'I been lookin' for you,' he said, his voice thick and rasping. 'You were there, when we rode through the rain, when we stopped at the big oak. You were there when they put the rope around my neck. I remember your face. I said I'd come back.'

'Shine. Oleg Shine,' Truckle stuttered, the dread, cracking his voice. 'You don't look like you did.'

'I lost some pounds. Hair turned an age. How'd you think you'd look after bein' hanged, then shot an' buried alive? My memory's still fair though.'

'How'd you get down?' Truckle asked, fearful and morbidly interested.

'I got my hands unticd. Most o' you were too damn cowardly to watch, or had rode off. I had a knife, an' managed to cut the rope. For a while I thought I was free.'

Truckle backed off to the edge of his table. His shoulders slumped and his legs were unsteady. 'What do you mean?'

'One o' you came back. I couldn't see his face.'

Shine took a step into the office. Truckle flinched, but the man stayed near the door, as if to guard his way out. 'It was the darkest night, but he shot me down where I lay. He was so sure he'd killed me that time. He rolled me into a shallow scrape with no more'n a shovelful o' dirt to cover me. He wanted the coyotes to finish his dirty work.'

'You got yourself out though.'

'Oh yeah. But it took me a time. I was hurt bad with the bullet wounds.'

'That was last Thanksgivin'. Why'd you wait so long before comin' back?'

'I was angry, real angry. I wanted that to go.'

Truckle felt vulnerable. 'Jesus, why should any one of us come back an' deliberately shoot, then bury you?' he asked.

'Because I was just the top hand o' the Blood Legs,' Shine said slowly. 'I figured out the man who came back was the leader. He tried to kill me because he was afraid I might talk.'

'How'd he know you weren't dead?'

'He didn't. He just wanted to make real sure. He'd have had a lot to lose if my tongue took to movin'.'

'That don't make sense. What's the point in him—?'

'You can call your friends out here,' Shine interrupted Truckle's rebuff.

Dan and Will stepped back into the office, their guns still holstered.

Shine considered them with his icy, penetrating stare. 'I seen you two before,' he said.

'We were fillin' our paunches in Ivy May's dinin'-room. You didn't stay long, I recall. I'm Dan Glass,

108

this is my brother Will.'

'You been back with the Blood Legs?' Will asked directly.

'No.' Shine was just as direct back. 'Not this time. But I hear they're up an' runnin' again.'

The man from a one-time chain gang then backed towards the door that led to the alley, his eyes continuing to hold the three men in the office. Without another word, and without seeming to move much, the door opened and closed and Shine was gone.

'That's a neat trick,' Will said. 'It's somethin' you an' me will have to work on.' For a moment or two there was no sound, save the soft guttering of the lamp on Truckle's desk. Then the chair creaked, as the big saloon owner stirred uneasily.

There was a grunt and a scuffle from the alley, and they all fixed their eyes on the door. Then the door flew open and Shine was standing there again. But this time, his face was contorted in a tight, painful grimace. He staggered back into the office.

'Oh, Jesus no,' Will groaned and quickly moved forward.

'Looks like I waited too long,' Shine gasped. 'Never get to finish the job now. You boys . . . you find out.' Then the man pitched forward, his long body sprawled face down on the thinly carpeted floor.

Dan leaped to the open door. With his Colt drawn, he half stepped into the deepy shadowed alley. There was no one there, but he thought he heard some-thing, and a breeze moved the chilly air.

'He won't be comin' back this time,' Will said,

kneeling beside Shine's body. 'They done for him, like Joe Dace.'

'Yeah, I can see,' Dan said, looking at the spike protruding from deep down in the dead man's back.

17

THE GUNMEN ARRIVE

Angry frustration swept over Will as he stared at the still figure of Oleg Shine. Cedar Truckle rose from his chair. He scowled, his features heavy and sweaty in the yellow light.

'Now, we got a job to do,' he said. 'Maybe I can repay him some by doin' it. I owe him that.'

'Yeah, you do,' Will agreed sullenly. 'We're overlookin' the fact that you could still be a leader o' them Blood Legs. He never quite cleared that up, did he?'

'I ain't forgot.' Truckle glared at Will defiantly. 'But him gettin' skewered like that kind o' proves I ain't.'

'Maybe,' Will said, thoughtfully.

'There ain't no "maybe" about it, more's the pity,' a self-important voice growled from the alley door.

With two of his gunslicks in the alley behind him, their guns at the ready, Rafer Vorn stood watching the three men in the saloon-keeper's office. He stepped into the crowded room, his men moving forward to either side of the door.

'It would take one to know one,' Will said coolly. 'An' one to know he ain't.'

'Well, there'll be no chance to spread what *you* know,' Vorn said, the scorn plain to hear. 'I ain't forgot what happened out at the Long G.'

'Nor have we,' Dan answered back. 'An' the Chappel kid ain't either. I told you what I'd do the next time we met, Vorn.'

'Ha, says the man with his pants around his knees,' Vorn sneered. 'You ain't in a position to threaten anybody.'

'An' you ain't goin' to shoot all three of us,' Truckle spoke up. 'Whichever o' these boys goes down first, the other one'll get you. If they don't I will,' he warned.

'How the hell you goin' to do that, Truckle. Goin' to try a long spit?'

'Nope. From under this desk, I'm levellin' an old Dragoon Colt. One o' your men pulls a trigger, an' only the top half o' you gets buried.'

But Dan was tired of the talking. 'There's somethin' I want settled before we start shootin',' he said intolerantly. 'I'm a man o' my word, so get outside, Vorn,' he rasped. Then he stepped forward, glared at Vorn and unbuckled his gunbelt.

'Hmm. Well, with you out of the way that'll just leave these two gun-happies,' Vorn crowed. 'That's a fair match for me and my boys.'

'You know what you're doin'?' Will asked, as his brother went by him, shrugging off his coat.

'Nope, an' I'm hopin' he don't either.' Then Dan stepped into the alley and held out his arms. 'What we waitin' for?' he asked calmly.

Vorn removed his coat, folded it once and handed it to one of his gunnies. He flexed his fingers, balled his fists, and rushed out at Dan.

Dan went into a crouch. In a driving lunge, he took Vorn just above the knees, raised his back as he felt the contact. Vorn lost his grip and his footing. He went high, twisted over Dan's back. He tried to break his fall, but failed and landed heavily on his shoulder and face in the dark, stinking ground. He loosed off a big grunt of air, swore and got to his feet.

Dan held his hands down, watched Vorn carefully.

A low, angry noise rose up in Vorn's throat. Thinking out his move, he came in guardedly, but then reckless. Dan landed a punch in the front meat of his face, went inside with it, and gave him a hard shoulder in the chest. Then he stepped nimbly aside, chopped Vorn across his ear with the edge of his hand, as the man lunged past him.

But Vorn kept his balance. He turned on his heel, and came back fast. His arms were whirling and his breath was coming in guttural soughs.

Dan knew that Vorn had a reach advantage of a few inches. He knew too, that if he kept on at Vorn's face, the man would get stirred to murderous strength. So, it was the belly that he aimed for. With his left hand in the crook of Vorn's elbow, it checked the man's movement long enough for him to pivot inside his body. He lifted a driving right into the middle of Vorn's shirt, felt the jarring impact of a jawbone on the point of his shoulder.

He broke away, veered and ducked at Vorn's reach for a bear hug. But Vorn thought it was a retreat, and charged stubbornly.

Dan was quick and ready, and Vorn walked into Dan's straight left arm. It stopped Vorn with a jolt that set him straight from the knees upwards. Dan saw his opening and heaved in a wild right with his weight behind it. He felt his fist go deep and low into Vorn's belly, at the same time caught Vorn's knuckled haymaker on the side of his forehead. It put him down, and with his head making bell noises, he rolled once and clambered to his feet.

Dan stood hurting and breathless. Vorn was flat on his back, his arms wrapped around his belly, his knees doubled to his chin. He was sucking air with an ugly sob. Dan walked over to him, was only then aware of the men who stood silent and stunned in the light of the doorway.

He turned his attention back to Rafer Vorn. The man from Short Snake rolled on to his knees, retched and came shakily to his feet, his back to Dan.

'This way, Vorn. Won't be long now,' Dan said breathlessly.

Vorn swung around heavily, his feet spread to brace himself. He had grazes on his face and a cut lip that was bleeding, glistening in the murk. He wiped his cheek on his shirt, heaved his chest with the effort of breathing.

'You can walk away,' Dan offered.

Vorn sensed a blood gobbet on his chin, and he wiped it away with an angry gesture. For ten long seconds, he regarded Dan with loathing in his eyes. Then, slowly, he staggered over to the man with his coat. He pulled it away with his left hand, took a revolver from the other gunman with his right.

The men were surprised, momentarily distracted. They turned to see a shooting, but Will and Truckle had seen Vorn's tactic. Will drew his Colt, and before Vorn had a chance to put a bullet into Dan, he was falling, nearly dead with two bullets tearing up the side of his face.

Dan took a couple of long, deep breaths. 'I got that all wrong,' he said, staring numbly at Vorn's blood-spattered body. 'For a moment there, it was you doin' the scarin'.'

Truckle had pulled down the Winchester he kept above the door. He levered a shell into the breech, was itching for a target. He glared at the two gunmen. 'So much as a sniffle and you die,' he said, without a trace of smile.

Will stepped between them, a cold glitter in his eyes. 'My brother has probably got it into his head that you two pigeons are here to do Vorn's dirty work. So, while he dusts himself off, you're goin' to coo,' he said grimly. 'Vorn as good as told us his outfit was part of the Blood Legs. Well, was he? Was he the boss?'

'No,' one of the men said quickly. 'Rafer got his

orders an' passed 'em down.'

'Who was the big augur then?' Will pressured.

'We don't know,' said the other gunman. 'We had no interest in knowin'. We ain't from this territory. We did it for the money.'

Buckling his gunbelt back on, Dan was considering what form of reprisal to mete out, when the inside door leading from Truckle's office started to be hammered on with someone's fist.

'Hey, you all right, Cedar?' called a voice that Dan and Will thought they recognized. 'What's the shootin'?'

Will nodded at Truckle, who went to the inner door and unlocked it. He pulled it open, confronted Elam Medows who was standing there with the barkeep who enjoyed trouble.

'What the hell!' Medows exclaimed, looking around quickly.

'Yeah, we been havin' some trouble,' Truckle said. 'That's Oleg Shine lyin' there. Vorn's outside.'

Medows was shocked. 'Shine?' he repeated. 'He came back? The dead man, actually came back?'

'Not for long. An' there's a story to it. Somebody stuck him in the alley.'

'Well, it weren't us,' one of the gunmen claimed. 'An' we didn't see anyone else either.'

'What happened to Vorn? Who shot him?' the callous barkeep wanted to know.

'I did,' Will told him. 'He wanted to backshoot Dan. He was a Blood Leg an' a miserable cur. Take your pick.'

'Did he tell you who's headin' up them dogs?'

Medows asked next.

'No, but we know it weren't Shine.'

'That's too bad,' Medows reflected grimly. 'Let's hope we find out before there's too many more killin's.'

18

THE CALL TO ARMS

In less than ten minutes from Will's shooting of Rafer Vorn, Amos Hatte appeared with the Northport deputies. Richmond Cord and Nestor Midland were in meddlesome, close attendance.

'I know what you're thinkin',' Dan muttered to his brother, as the group jostled in the doorway.

'Yeah. Another good time to rob the bank,' Will voiced, on the brink of loudness.

Hatte was carrying an aged scattergun. He scowled as he pushed his way in, saw Truckle's Winchester covering the two gunmen.

'I shoulda known it was you two,' he grated, on seeing Dan and Will. 'I suppose you'll want to be deputized next. What's happened here?'

Truckle quickly explained all that had happened during the last ten minutes.

'Well, there's nothin' in any o' that, that convinces me that these two aren't the leaders of the Blood Legs,' Midland snorted. 'What about Coddle's note, an' the chain link, that was found on 'em? This town needs more proficient law enforcement, an' I'll certainly be bringin' that forward before the next election.'

'Ah, shut your mouth, Midland!' Truckle yelled. 'None of us wants to listen to your piss an wind.'

'*You* shut up!' Midland bellowed back. 'You seem to think you rule the roost around here. These men were helped in their jail break, an' I want to know by whom.'

'The *whom* was me,' Truckle said calmly. 'I gave Will Glass a gun, warned both of 'em to get out of town. You an' Medows were raisin' up the whole o' Wyandot. There's some of us who've had enough o' lynchin' parties.'

'That's a goddamn lie,' snapped Medows. 'I wasn't part of any such doin'.'

'Huh. The losin' horse blamin' the saddle,' Dan muttered, and Will smiled thinly.

'I've heard enough,' the sheriff said, and grinned at Will. 'You think I wouldn'ta come after you, if I'd thought you guilty?'

'I had wondered.' Will attempted a smile, and eased his Colt back into his holster.

Amos Hatte looked openly at Will. 'I figured you an' your brother would learn a lot more'n me,' he said. 'An' you did. You found Oleg Shine, an' you found out that Vorn was in league with the Blood Legs.'

'Nearly right, Sheriff. It was Shine that found us,' Dan corrected Hatte.

Hatte nodded thoughtfully, told the deputies to take Vorn's gunmen off to the jail. 'An' someone take charge o' the dead men,' he said to no one in particular.

For a short while, and undeterred, Nestor Midland continued to bicker. Medows was suddenly gone and no one else was interested. He snorted his disgust, stomped from the office towards the main street.

'Well, Sheriff,' Truckle said, 'I suggest we round up some men.'

'Yeah. Ready to ride at first light,' Will added.

'I figured it was time somebody thought o' that,' Cord said sharply. The stable keeper then walked off into the darkness, said he'd grab a few hours' sleep.

Will tossed Truckle's revolver on to the desk, leaned his back tiredly against the wall. 'I'd like to have my own gun back again, Sheriff,' he said. 'Goes for Dan, too.'

'It goes for *all* of us,' Hatte said, with a sly glance at Dan. 'I don't reckon this cannon's been fired since the Revolution. Stop by the office, an' I'll return 'em.'

Dan glanced at the sheriff's empty holster and grinned, handed over the .45. 'Yeah, a real nice piece. Thanks for the use of it,' he said.

Will held up his hand for their attention at the sound of hoofs from the street. 'That's a vital assignment,' he said. 'I just wonder where it'll be at this hour?'

Dan was of the same mind. 'Whoever it is, they're

ridin' with the wind up their ass. We don't stand much chance o' catchin' him.'

'I figure we should do somethin' about it,' Hatte said. 'But it's knowin' what.'

'I'm sure they don't call you the 'lets see how it goes' sheriff for nothin, Amos,' Truckle said with a wry grin. 'But this time, let's not wait for the mornin'. Will's right. Let's round up every man we can get. Meet the trouble that's surely comin'. I've an idea who that rider might be, but I ain't about to say. My heart ain't in fingerin' the wrong man any more.'

'There's somethin' to what you say,' Hatte said. 'But if the Blood Legs know they're on a short rope, they're likely to try an' clean out the whole basin, an' fast. What's the best way o' roundin' up these helpin' folk?'

'Send one o' your deputies to the Banded Wing an' another to Nitch Gordam,' Dan replied. 'Have 'em warned to be ready for trouble.'

'As if they aren't already,' Will added.

'I'll wake up every man in town that can be trusted. So it shouldn't take too long,' Truckle said with a dry smile. 'What about you, Will?'

'Get our horses from Cord an' pick up our guns from the sheriff's office. We'll head for the Short Snake and Rafer Vorn, since we're reckonin' on that bein' the headquarters of the Blood Legs.'

'You won't go ridin' in?'

'No. We'll keep watch, be ready to ride and warn the town if they head this way.'

'Dan'll ride with you?'

'Well, he can speak for himself, but he'll go where

I go. It's somethin' he's been doin' all our lives.'

The four men separated, the sheriff heading for his office to give orders to his deputies, Truckle to rouse the townsmen he trusted.

Before Will and Dan hurried off to the livery stable for their horses, Will wagged a finger at Truckle. 'You don't really keep a gun under your desk, do you?' he asked, with a crafty grin.

'Yeah, 'course I do. Take a look.'

Will and Dan looked at each other, kneeled to peer beneath the desk. There in the shadow they saw the massive old Colt. It was in a gunbelt that had been nailed to the underside of the table top.

'It ain't loaded though,' Truckle said, and gave an exaggerated wink.

Will and Dan hurried along to the livery stable, but the place was locked and deserted. When they pounded on the door there was no answer.

'You think this is the stable door that got locked *before* the horse got bolted?' Dan wondered.

'Yes, I'm sure,' Will indulged his brother. 'Let's try another way.'

19

THE TRACK WEST

The two men hurried around to the rear of the stable. The back door was closed, but Dan had a way. He took one step back and served up his reliable heel. The door gave and they were inside within a moment. There was an oil lantern burning, but most of the stable was in the gloom. From the stalls, a horse kicked, jerked nervously at its strap line.

'Nobody here but them an' us,' Dan observed.

Will and Dan got their horses from the stalls, saddled them up, and led them out through the back door that was hanging from its hinges.

'What neck o' the woods we goin' to find the Short Snake in?' Dan wanted to know, as he swung into the saddle.

'The western end o' the basin, to the south,' Will said.

From collecting their Colts at the sheriff's office, they rode west to pick up the wagon road. They'd gone a mile past the town's grave patch, when a rider emerged from the shadows beneath a low-spreading creekside oak.

'Leavin' the basin?' Jasper Stebbs challenged, and thrust his rifle at them. 'Best idea you had since arrivin'.'

'What the hell does it matter to you where we're goin', Stebbs?' Will asked angrily. 'You know what happened to the last piece o' garbage that jumped us?'

'I'm a lot smarter,' Stebbs crowed. 'An' I aim to keep it that way.'

'An' I'm real angered with people pullin' guns on me, gettin' punched, an' bein' told to move on,' Dan blasted back. 'Now, if you want, go ahead an' pull the trigger o' that smoke pole, 'cause dyin' ain't too smart.'

There was a short, intense wait, then Stebbs's eyes gave him away. They flickered, moved a fraction to his right, as Will flicked the reins of his sabino.

It was all that Dan needed. He drew and put a bullet straight into Stebbs's chest, then another fast round, as the body jerked in the saddle.

Stebbs looked futilely at Dan. His eyes tried to blink away the cloudiness and the pain. His fingers were numb and he couldn't get off the shot he desperately wanted to. 'Hurts, too,' he gasped, and let go of his rifle, took a final, short gulp of air and followed it to the dirt.

Dan sat waiting for the fall. He thrust his gun back into the holster and swung out of the saddle. It took a moment, nothing more than a hasty glance to know that Stebbs was dead.

Stebbs's mount had wandered over to the side of the road, and it stood there waiting, its dark coat shiny in the looming darkness.

'He had it comin' to him, Dan,' Will said. 'There'da been a next time.'

But Dan had already reasoned Stebbs's death. 'What now? We still headin' for the Short Snake?' he wanted to know.

'Yeah. When you tidied up the mess you made.'

Dan dragged the body to the side of the road. 'People don't always die the way they should in Lobo Basin. But you seem to have done OK,' he said harshly. Then he went to Stebbs's horse. He picked up the reins and tied them loosely to the saddle horn. He gave the animal a slap on its flank and it trotted away, headed for the corral at Banded Wing.

'They'll probably send out a rider.' Dan was almost dismissive. He remounted and together they continued riding west along the wagon road towards the Vorn spread.

'Thanks for creatin' that disturbance, Will,' Dan said, after a few minutes. 'Do you think Stebbs was out for us?' he asked.

'Not entirely. He couldn'ta known we were comin' this way. I reckon he was here protectin' the ass of whoever rode from town. It musta been important for him to shoot dead anyone chasin' 'em.'

'Yeah. But I guess *we* must know whatever *they* did,' Dan supposed.

'That the ranchers are getting' together? Risin' up for a fight back?'

'Yeah, amongst other things. Like Oleg Shine not bein' a runner. Rafer Vorn cashin' in his chips.'

'Yeah. An' us bein' in the middle again. Don't forget that, Will.'

'There's one thing for sure: Stebbs won't be brow-beatin' Fearon Chappel any more. Whatever their trouble was, it ain't any longer. Not that Chappel knows that,' Will said. 'I wonder if Stebbs was a member of the Blood Legs?' was an added thought.

'I guess we just made him one,' Dan said.

The two riders left the wagon road and headed further across the open rangeland towards the western end of the basin.

'There's one thing still puzzlin' me,' Dan said, thoughtfully. 'All this trouble must have somethin' to do with that railroad deal. Nothin' else makes much sense.'

'That's true. I been thinkin' the same. Vorn seems to have been second-in-command so he'd be one to gain, I guess. The Short Snake's big, but ain't in the same league as the others. If the rail spur runs across the basin, it'll go through land that's owned by Dace, Chappel *and* Gordam. But it won't be touchin' Vorn's. They'll be bendin' north to Roscoe or Brule before that.'

'Yeah. So Vorn makes nothin' from the railroad. But he would, an' mountains of it, if he owned the others. That's where the big settlement money is. Right?'

'Makes a heap o' sense, Dan. Just needed some puttin' together.'

The land began to change as they moved further

west. Towards the border country, the grass turned thinner, the ground more uneven, broke frequently into hogbacks and gullies. It was from around one of these ridges that the riders appeared ahead of them. There was six of them, and they wore an assortment of neck-cloths across the lower parts of their faces. They were all armed and they didn't speak or exchange commands. But for Will and Dan, there was concern in the way they spread as they rode forward.

'I don't suppose that now's the time to tell you that there are times when I don't want to follow you everywhere,' Dan said resignedly.

20

THE ROUND UP

Neither Dan nor Will made an attempt on their guns. They'd get blasted before they cleared leather. Without fuss, the six horsemen surrounded them, continued with their menacing silence. Will and Dan halted their mounts, sat their saddles waiting.

One of the men rode close to Dan's right, reached out and drew his Colt from the holster. Another, who'd edged his horse to Will, did the same.

'I know these fellers,' said another of the masked men. 'They're the shootists. Call 'emselves the Glass brothers.'

'I heard. It was them that shot Vorn,' said the man who'd taken Will's gun.

'I can hardly believe this is happenin',' Dan muttered. 'Is that a good or bad move for us?' he asked.

The man didn't answer. But another said for them

all to move out. 'The boss'll be real keen to see 'em,' he said.

Will knew then that they'd be all right, at least until they got there. He let his chin fall to his chest, closed his eyes and let the sabino follow on. He didn't look back, but guessed Dan would probably do the same. There wasn't after all, much to talk about.

But it was talk that brought Will to. He looked up to see the shapes of low buildings huddled in the darkness ahead, realized they'd reached Vorn's Short Snake ranch.

Will noticed that there were many horses in the corrals, more than an outfit working on a ranch this size would need. Lights gleamed through the windows of the main building and the bunkhouse had yellow squares that cut the night.

'You folk sure keep late hours,' Dan said. 'Horses conduct a lot of their business at night, do they? Most honest folk are in the land o' nod by now,' he added a little carelessly.

'Keep your mouth workin', mister,' one of the riders answered. 'Give it a final run out.'

The eight riders reached the front of the ranch house and halted their mounts. A stern-faced man stepped from the front doorway, his features silhouetted by the lamplight behind him.

'What you boys brought in?' he asked.

'We rounded up some strays. Go by the names o' Glass,' said one of the masked riders, as he swung down from his horse. 'The boss here?'

'Yeah,' said the man on the porch. 'I'll see if he wants 'em brought in through.'

'Mind if we climb down?' Will said. 'Unless you want us to ride in. We obviously ain't goin' anywhere.'

'Go ahead,' the man said, palming the butt of his high-belted Colt.

Dan and Will swung from their saddles, let their reins fall. They were mindful of the men around them. Four were still in their saddles, two now stood near the veranda steps.

'Boss says for the two o' you to bring 'em in,' the man said, on returning. 'You other men saddle up fresh horses. Be ready to ride within the hour.'

'What road we guardin' this time?' asked one of the men near the steps.

'You ain't; you're ridin' to Wyandot,' said the man standing above them. 'Now, let's get them Vorn killers up here.'

Will started up the steps with Dan by his side. The others dismounted and led all the horses bar a sorrel to the nearby corral. The man in the doorway took a long look out into the darkness as Will and Dan crossed the veranda, took a step back as they entered the lighted hallway with the two watchful guards.

Towards the rear of the house, there was a door that was half open. Will went up to it, stopped outside the small, comfortable-looking study.

A man was sitting at a leather-topped writing-desk. The light from an ornately engraved oil lamp shone across his dark broadcloth suit, white shirt, string tie. He held his hands beneath the desk, redolent of Cedar Truckle and the Dragoon Colt.

'Well, if it ain't the dude who warned us about

stayin' in Wyandot. I guess we should've taken your advice,' Dan said, looking coldly at Elam Medows.

Curiously, Will found that the first thing he thought of as he stood there, was the man's interest in Ivy May. Elam Medows was a gambler, but if he was wanting her hand, being the leader of a gang of land thieves and murderers was a very bad bet.

Then Will recalled someone saying that it was Midland and Medows who were shouting for the necks of him and his brother. Suddenly staying alive was an option for him to consider seriously.

Medows looked up at the stern-faced man who'd stood on the veranda as they pulled up.

'You know what the orders are, Mink,' Medows said. 'You go now. Kiss Wyandot goodbye for me.'

'Sure, Boss,' the man called Mink said. Then he turned to leave with the two men who were still wearing their bandannas across their faces, eased the door to behind them.

Medows noticed the fading smile on Will's face. 'What you got to be so pleased about?' he asked.

'Because I don't reckon you're the one who's callin' the shots here. This is a set-up.'

'Come in an' tell me what the hell you're talkin' about,' Medows said, with a lean smile.

Will realized then that they hadn't been left alone. There was another man in the room with Medows. He was sitting on the end of a Davenport with a walnut-stocked scattergun across his knees. He was wearing a tattered executioner's hood, and Will shuddered.

'I gave you that advice for your own good,' Medows said, looking at Dan as he spoke. 'Now look at the mess you got yourself in, by not heedin' me.'

Will took a step closer to Medows, but with a hushed rasp in his throat, the other man called for him to hold up.

Will held up his hands in compliance. 'You sure made it here fast, Medows,' he said. 'It musta been you leavin' town, an' it weren't much ahead of us.'

Medows assumed a sudden, nervous expression. 'I went lookin' for her. She weren't—' he started to say.

'Shut it,' the whispering man commanded abruptly. 'That's enough.'

From outside, a baffled Will and Dan heard the soft pounding of horses' hoofs, guessed it would be the Blood Legs heading out for Wyandot.

A sense of futility swept over Will as he remembered telling Cedar Truckle and the sheriff that they'd warn the town if and when the raiders were coming.

'Get your hands above the table, Medows,' Will said. 'I got reason to feel nervous with you sittin' like that.'

Medows raised an eyebrow, then his hands. 'See, nothin to worry about,' he said. showing that his hands were tightly bound.

21

THE NARROW ESCAPE

'You goddamn fool,' the hooded man rasped, finding it hard to retain his whisper. 'I warned about you playin' this some other way,' he said, getting to his feet.

'Don't worry. You ain't let the cat out o' the bag,' Will said, staring at Medows's bound wrists. 'I already told you, I reckon this is a set-up. The Blood Leg general ain't likely to be sittin' there without his hood. We picked that much up from one or two of his foot soldiers, before they died.'

The hooded man's pale eyes bore chillingly into Will. It was a moment of trigger tension and nobody paid much attention to Dan. He was standing off a little, and they didn't see him reach inside his shirt and draw out a revolver.

'You ain't sure who to drop, mister. I am, an' it

gives me the edge,' he snapped. 'Drop the scatter-gun, or do it while you're dyin'.'

The hooded man turned slowly to face Dan, saw the dogged set of his face. He grunted and drooped the big barrels of his gun. But only so far. He, too, took advantage of the split second of unease. He whirled his arms and smashed the oil lamp with the tip of the shotgun. In the immediate and intense darkness, it dashed across the floor towards Dan's feet.

Will dropped to the floor with the expected blast of gunfire resounding madly in the close confines of the room. He knew there'd be another blast, then doubted it. The man would keep that for a second chance if he needed it.

To force the issue, Will got to his feet, but saw the man's shape filling the window opening as he went through and away.

Dan fired, but it was too late and he missed easy. A moment later they all heard the pounding of boots along the front veranda. Then the excited snorting of the sorrel, the hoofbeats as it took flight.

'That was the man you're after, that we're *all* after,' came Medows's voice from the darkness. 'An' at that clip, he'll be holed up by the side o' Lake McConoughy by mid-mornin'.'

Dan found his way to the door. He went out to the hall to fetch an oil lamp, brought it back into the den. He still had the gun in his free hand, and he dropped it into his empty holster.

'Where'd you get that iron?' Will asked him.

'In the alley. I took it out o' Vorn's hand. Everyone

was watchin' you, after shootin' him.'

Dan put the lamp down on the desk. He caught the clasp-knife that Will tossed him and cut the ropes that bound Elam Medows's wrists.

'It was Ivy May you were talkin' about earlier, wasn't it?' Will said. 'I'm guessin' it was Vorn that had her taken. Which was why you headed out here in such a hurry. How near to the truth's that?'

'Close enough,' said Medows, rubbing one wrist, then the other. 'I discovered she was missin' soon as I got back to her place after leavin' Truckle's office.'

'Too much to suppose you know who he is?' Will asked speculatively. 'Did he say or do *anythin'* to give you a lead on his identity? Somethin' to make you think?'

Medows shook his head. 'No, nothin'. One minute I got him buttonholed, next minute he's all the folk I ever met. We must know him though, otherwise he'd use a normal voice, instead o' that goddamn throat snuffle.'

'Oh, we know him all right,' Dan said, artfully.

Medows considered his next few words. 'So, you're OK with me an' Miss Ivy, are you, Glass?' he said. 'One time I thought I saw an interest.'

'Yeah, I'm OK with it,' Will said, not entirely at ease with his response.

'An' I'm goin' to be OK when we get the hell out o' this place,' Dan said. 'I don't care much for still bein' here when them sackheads come back.'

Will went over to a high cabinet that was fitted in one corner of the room. He turned a key and pulled open the double doors. 'Here we are,' he said, taking

135

in the revolvers and rifles stacked inside. 'I think it's help yourself.'

'Yeah, an' we're goin' to need 'em,' Dan agreed. He selected a .44 army revolver and stuffed it behind the buckle of his pants belt.

Medows picked up a .36 calibre Manhattan, examined it, and thrust it into a shoulder holster he wore beneath his coat. 'An' now, I guess we're wastin' time,' he said eagerly. 'I got a feelin' maybe they brought Ivy here.'

'Here? You think they actually brought her *here*? Why the hell didn't you mention it before,' Will flashed out. 'Where do you reckon she'll be?'

'Upstairs. It's too busy down here. Too close.'

They went back into the hall and looked around them, out through the open doorway. There was no movement, and Medows led the way up the stairs to the upper floor. Bristling with firearms, Will and Dan followed him.

There was a small wall sconce burning at the head of the stairway, threw their wavy shadows along a broad corridor. At the end, a door stood open and more light came from the room beyond.

The three men walked directly to the door, peered into a bedroom where Ivy May was lying on the bed. Her hands and feet were tied, her hair was mussed and her face glistened wet from the crying.

Will gallantly pushed into the room. 'Sorry we're late, miss,' he said, with good humour. 'Mister Medows forgot to mention that you might be here. But I guess he was preoccupied.'

Medows stepped in to quickly untie the ropes,

draw them away from Ivy's wrists and ankles. He smiled diffidently but warmly, and Ivy reciprocated with relief and an even bigger smile.

'How'd they get hold o' you?' he asked.

Ivy sat up on the bed, swung her legs to the ground. 'I went out back for some air, because the kitchen was so hot. That's when they grabbed me. They must have been waiting. They tied me up and put me on a blanket in the back of a buckboard. I didn't know where we were going. I'm so pleased to see you, Elam,' she said.

Medows put his arms around her, while Will and Dan shared an accepting, worldly look.

'They were wearin' hoods, weren't they?' Will asked, after a long moment.

Ivy nodded. 'I didn't see much of them. But, yes, they were,' she said.

'I think we should get out o' here,' Dan persisted.

Medows agreed. 'Yeah, before any of 'em decide to come back,' he said.

Ivy pushed herself from the bed and Dan had a quick look from the window.

'Can't see a goddamned thing,' he said. 'I hope they ain't out there, waitin'.'

The four of them were leaving the room when, from downstairs, a door banged into its frame.

'Who the hell. . . ?' Dan turned to Will, but his brother was ahead of him, already at the head of the stairs.

'I can smell it. It's the oil,' he said. He pulled his gun and started down the stairs, pumping bullets into the darkness below.

Then, the flames appeared. First, small yellow waves, then a fiercer, rolling cloud of red and gold.

'They've torched the place,' Will yelled. 'Get down here quick. There'll be a way out back.'

22

THE NIGHT FLIGHT

On the lower floor now, the flames spread quickly as they licked at the oil-soaked floor. They caught the foot of the stairs and began to creep upward.

But Will, Dan, Ivy May and Elam Medows were down and away, through the big rear doors at the back of the house.

'Did you see anyone?' Dan asked Will, as for a moment they looked back at the burning.

'No one,' Will said. 'Someone came back though. That door bangin' was them leavin'.'

'Yeah. Let's go see the horses,' Dan recommended eagerly.

They headed for the harness shed, which was far enough from the house not to be in any danger of catching a spark from the fire. They found saddles, bridles, blankets and the other rigging they needed. When they reached the corral, Dan called out with relief.

'Our horses are here, Will. They're saddled an' ready, as we left 'em.'

Dan roped a horse apiece for Ivy and Medows, then they gathered the gear and saddled up.

Dan looked determinedly at his brother. 'We know where to go now,' he said. 'I'm plain tired o' that scum takin' a pop at us. We'll never get out o' this territory, unless we go meet 'em.'

'I know,' Will said, already moving off his sabino as he swung into the saddle.

They rode from the corral, leaving the gate open. The horses balked as the back end of the house's roof gave way and the gun cabinet went up. They flicked their legs, went into a run, and the riders let them go.

After they'd raced two miles in the direction of Wyandot, the horses slowed to a steady trot.

'What time is it?' Dan asked.

'Without lookin' at my watch, I'd say no later than three,' Will said.

They rode on in silence and within an hour they found themselves on the wagon road that led to town. They encountered no one during their journey, the rangeland seemed ominously quiet.

The buildings of Wyandot were dark outlines; at such an early hour, there was no sign of movement in the town.

'That's strange. From the way they talked, I was certain the Blood Legs were comin' in here tonight,' Will said.

Medows closed his horse alongside Dan's bayo. 'Remember me tellin' Mink to raze the town?' he asked.

'Yeah, We remember,' Dan answered him. 'Maybe they did. Maybe there's no one left alive.'

'I've got some lamps still burning,' Ivy said.

Slow and quiet, they rode into the deserted main street, reined in outside of Ivy May's Rooms. They all dismounted, Will and Dan loose-tying their mares to the hitching rail.

Ivy and Medows led the way up and into the lobby, where the oil lamps had been turned low. Ivy's night clerk was dozing at the desk, and he was taken aback, looked very miserable. Cedar Truckle's voice hailed them as they came in.

'You got through. They let you in.' Truckle, advanced on them, grinning with a sort of relief. His Winchester was clutched tight in his nervy hands.

'What do you mean?' Will asked. 'Let us in, where?'

'They've got the town surrounded,' Truckle said. 'Been that way for the past two hours. They've been lettin' folk in. Those that try an' leave, get shot.'

'How many's that then?' Dan asked.

'We brought three in, so far.'

'I suddenly changed my mind about gettin' away from here,' Dan was heard to mutter.

'Who's in town?' Will asked.

'Just about all who live here, I guess. A few from the ranches.'

Dan turned to look back out of the door. 'Are the streets safe?' he asked of Truckle.

'So far.'

Will looked from Ivy to Medows, then back at Truckle. 'Hatte's deputies should have warned

Chappel an' Gordam by now. With no trouble out there, they might head back here, to see what's goin' on,' he told them. 'They could find a way through an' out again. They got the numbers.'

'Yeah, let's hope,' Truckle said.

Dan looked at the eager faces. 'If they're still here at daybreak, we might be able to see 'em. Give us a idea o' their layout, their weak points,' he said hopefully.

'Hmm. We ain't in any danger here an' now,' Will advised. 'So, why not all of us get our heads down. Well, at least some of us.'

'I'm gone,' Ivy said.

Medows waved his arm out towards the stairs. 'Yeah, you deserve it more'n most,' he said. 'I'll keep Cedar here up to date on the night's happenin's.'

Will nodded. 'An' we'll take care o' the horses.'

'Thanks,' said Ivy and Medows.

Out front, Will and Dan swung back into their saddles, took the reins of the other two horses from Medows.

'See you shortly,' said Will, and the pair rode off towards the livery stable.

'You know that friends are lost by callin' often,' Richmond Cord said, on seeing them.

'You just open up, Cord, then go back to sleep. Pretend you dreamed the whole thing,' Dan called through the small, side door.

Lazily, Cord got to his feet. The big front door opened after a while, and Will and Dan rode their horses through.

'You just leave 'em there. I'll take care o' the unsaddlin'.' Cord said. 'To be honest, I'm dead sick o' the sight o' you two. Trouble's only a few feet behind you . . . treadin' on your tails.'

Dan shrugged and left the stable with his brother, headed back towards Ivy May's. It was an ominous, chilling walk, knowing that armed killers were lurking somewhere out in the darkness.

Will knew that in time, whoever was leading the group of desperate men would grow impatient. Then they'd ride in, bring the attack right into town, to the very back yards of its citizens, if they had a mind to.

'What I'd give to know who's headin' up that scurvy pack,' Dan said. 'It's so close. He's so familiar, I can almost smell him. He was the one who came back an' set fire to the Short Snake, wasn't he?'

'Yeah, 'course it was,' Will said.

They walked on in silence, had almost reached Ivy May's when a figure loomed out of the shadows. Amos Hatte stood blocky on the boardwalk in front of them.

'That's a dumb move,' Dan gasped, his Colt already in his hand. 'I coulda blasted you back to your office.'

'Where'd you come from?' the sheriff demanded officiously.

'Right now, we come from the livery. Why?' Will asked, pushing his own Colt back.

'Them Blood Legs have got the town surrounded.'

'Yeah, we know.'

'I ain't got a taste for this anymore, fellers,' he

said, his manner tired and already half beat. 'I took this post 'cause it was civic. For me, the fightin' days are over. I'm just playin' a role . . . don't know what to do.'

'Leave it to us then,' Dan said confidently. 'If all else fails, we'll just play I-Spy, an' wait for your deputies to ride in with reinforcements.'

23

THE LINE OF DEFENCE

The three men went straight to the jailhouse. The sheriff locked the door and drew the blinds. He lighted a smeary oil lamp and seated himself at his desk, motioned Will and Dan to a pair of hard-back chairs.

'Now, tell me what happened?' he asked.

Will briefly explained how they'd been captured and taken to Vorn's ranch. How they'd found Elam Medows being forced to act as the leader of the Blood Legs, what had happened when they'd rode for Wyandot. He told of Ivy May and of how they'd escaped, of the man who'd come back to fire the ranch house.

'An' you figure he was the one who leads 'em? The one who got away? You reckon he rode back here, to

145

Wyandot?' Hatte asked, dumbfounded.

'Oh yeah, I'm sure of it,' Will said. 'An' that some-how he'll be bringin' 'em in. But that ain't for you to get bothered about right now. Tell me, Sheriff, what's the matter with you an' the rest o' the men o' this town?'

'What do you mean?' Hatte bridled.

'A buch o' gunslicks surround the town. They shoot three o' your citizens, an' anyone who tries to leave collects a ticket to the Milky Way. Meantime, you paddle about all goosey.'

'Well, tell us what to do.' All of a sudden, there was a note of co-operation in the sheriff's voice.

Will nodded, started on his quickly considered advice. 'In an hour or so, it'll be daylight. We build a barricade. Get everyone from their sleep, or their hidin'. Get 'em on the street to pile up stuff. We only got time to build one, but I'm guessin' they'll be comin' in from the west end o' town. Use anythin' you can. Carts, wagons, barrels an' boxes, furniture, anythin'.'

'We'll station men with guns right across the street,' Dan chipped in. 'We'll give these sidewinders more'n blood on their legs.'

'Yeah, I could arrange that,' Hatte said.

'So we'll get started,' Dan advised sharply.

Quickly and efficiently, the men went from build-ing to building along the street, rousing the citizens, telling them what was to be done. No one argued, and soon there were rifles, carbines and shotguns, positioned behind all manner of mercantile and household goods. Through one or two trapdoored ceilings, men had themselves staked-out on the rooftops.

When Dan, Will and the sheriff had finished their individual tasks, they stood on the boardwalk, looked over the defences.

'They'll see it, an' turn back,' Hatte groused.

'No, they won't. This is a town initiative. We're gettin' ready for a bric-a-brac sale,' Dan told him.

Will gave a good-humoured curse. 'You told everyone? Got everythin' in place?' he asked Hatte.

'Yeah. I reckon.'

'Good. Because I reckon this is them comin' now. Hold on to your hats, fellers, we're in for a stormy start to the day.'

Fifteen minutes after first light broke across the Lobo Basin, a band of masked horsemen swept in to the western end of the town. The last of Will and Dan's shouted instructions were lost as the muffled thunder of more than twenty horses hurtled towards the barricade. They were in a skirmish line, their stirrups almost touching. Each man carried a rifle and they were less than fifty yards away. The flank riders were carrying flaming brea torches, which they hurled at the nearest buildings.

'Fire!' Will shouted.

On his words, the first crash of shooting from the town's defenders roared out. The smoke and stench of cordite swirled around them as flames stabbed from nearly a dozen guns. But Will held his fire. He was peering through a gap in the barricade, while Dan showed him that three men had already crashed from their saddles. He called for another volley, watched intently as only one other man fell.

With Dan following, Will then ran for the board-walk where Cedar Truckle was standing in the half light. He'd taken shelter behind one of the posts of a building's overhang, and Will and Dan took up their own kneeling positions.

The wild pounding of hoofs, the shouting and cursing of fighting men, the stench of cordite, the flashes of flame and the roaring of the shooting, merged to a bedlam. To Dan, it seemed a curiously long way off. He'd become detached, as if he were a general of the field, not a soldier of the foot.

He saw the horses of the attackers close on the barricade. Two of the defenders had taken fatal bullets. Another was crawling towards the boardwalk, bleeding from wounds in the head and shoulders. Another was stretched out on his back, and wouldn't likely shoot again.

Everything was too crowded, then, for anyone to take stock of small things. The surging line of horses came towards the barricade and leapt.

The Blood Legs were using six-guns now, the firing was point blank. Will knew they were counting on their single attack, that the defenders weren't long lasting. Whoever was leading them wanted the break-through.

Will started shooting as the first of the horsemen leapt the barricade. He saw his man go down, and Dan was doing likewise. Truckle was wearing a fixed sneer as he worked the lever action of his Winchester.

Man after man went down. Horses thrashed their

legs as they sprawled over, squealing with pain, adding to the din and confusion. The cordite fumes made breathing difficult, stung nostrils and mouths as it was breathed in.

Two hooded attackers made a dash for the board-walk, and Dan sent one of them down with a hole in the side of his head big enough to take a fist. For a split second it looked as if Medows was about to meet his end, but he ducked as the bullets crashed out from the Will's Colt. Dan leaped at the same time, grabbing the second man's knees. He rolled striking and kicking as they went down, knowing that he had to kill or be killed. Then Will shot the man point blank.

Medows straightened up. Breathing hard, he took shelter with Dan, whose face was glistening, looking as if at last he'd found something that he was good at.

The last of the hooded men were milling, whirling their horses, madly fighting for control. They were sending lead at the men on the ground, up at those who'd found vantage points from the rooftops. There were many riderless horses now, making things tough for the remainder of the Blood Legs. They were no longer fighting with the fury they'd displayed when they'd first galloped furiously down the street.

'We're scarin' 'em,' Amos Hatte yelled.

'Yeah, an' me,' Dan shouted back.

They were all making their shots count now. Then Dan's hammer fell on an empty chamber. Will's did the same, and the two of them started to reload.

At that moment, and from the same, western end of the street, another column of mounted men, advanced at the full gallop. They were a grim-faced bunch. They wore no masks, but were all heavily armed.

24

THE RECKONING

For five more minutes, a scene of unspeakable confusion reigned, with men kicking, gouging, knifing and shooting. The cries of the wounded and the screams of the horses mingled with the savage shouting of the combatants.

'Over there!' Will suddenly shouted, and pointed. He was watching a hooded man who'd been shouting orders ever since the shooting started. 'Recognize that sorrel? It's the goddamn, big chief, an' he's comin' for us, Dan.'

The man swung his mount towards Will and Dan, ran at them as though he knew his hour had come. His gun roared, and Dan felt the bullet pulse past his neck. But the man was now taking bullets from both the Glass brothers' guns. Still firing, he closed on Will, but it was too late. The sorrel pulled up when it felt its rider lose control, when it felt the horn of its saddle being pulled and a revolver fell to the ground.

'I shoulda taken you two when I had the chance. There's been a few,' the rider gasped, as he fell across the boardwalk at the feet of Will.

'Yeah, I know,' Will said. 'An' the trouble's now trod on *your* wretched tail.'

In the street, the firing grew more sporadic. Wyandot men, ranchers and their waddies had won the encounter. The Blood Legs who weren't dead, or too badly wounded, were surrendering.

Assisted by the men and women of the town, the sheriff and his deputies went into action. Within a few minutes, the street was clearing of smoke, the fallen bodies, and smashed debris of the fight were being dragged away. Five prisoners had been hauled to the jail.

'They'll be standin',' Hatte called out. 'Use your boot an' a jimmy to get 'em in.'

Will and Dan had one last job to do. Will didn't want to spoil the occasion for anyone. So they took an arm apiece, dragged the wounded leader of the Blood Legs back across the street, down to the Beaker's Brim saloon.

Already inside, were Cedar Truckle, Fearon Chappel, Nitch Gordam and Elam Medows.

'Opened early for a good reason,' Truckle announced. 'Who is it you got there? We been takin' bets.'

'Let the coon see the hounds,' Chappel rasped.

Will pulled at the dirt-riddled hood that covered the features of the fatally wounded outlaw. Startled exclamations came from the men gathered around, as first the grizzled chin, then the dark stubs of teeth appeared in the blood-drained face of Richmond Cord.

'Jesus. So he's the gift we all been waitin' for,' Hatte exclaimed, in the outburst of crude epithets. 'There's me thinkin' he'd got animal dirt for brains.'

'Yeah, you an' most o' the town,' Truckle said, with a sickened voice.

Cord glared evilly at the men surrounding him. 'That's their problem,' he croaked.

'It was you killed Oleg Shine was it?' Will demanded. 'An' Joe Dace?'

'Yeah, left that iron link in Dace's maw to make you think Shine was back from the dead. Ha! Worked too . . . got you all makin' up your own crackpot stories. But he might o' worked it out, like you did, Glass. He was the only one I ever had to do in twice.' Cord's pale, watery eyes then closed.

Dan turned away to look hard at Will. 'You said you figured who he was. How did you know?' he asked.

Will kept his eyes on Cord's face. He wanted the man's eyes to open again, to see the expression of anger or bitterness.

'I recognized the shotgun,' he said. 'It's a fine Manton, made in London, England. Not the sort a liveryman usually carries. Then I recognized the sorrel. Saw it first when we collected them flea-bit greys. Then there was the .45 that Cedar handed me. It was Cord's idea though . . . his set up. Said to do it, 'cause o' the town gettin' ready to lynch us.'

Truckle's jaw dropped. He raised his head, then nodded very slowly. 'God yes, that was it,' he said, remembering. 'It was *this* murderous dog robber who arranged for you to be shot.'

'An' by knowin' it was him, you knew what end o' town they'd ride in from. They'd pick him up from the livery. It was *him* who planted that note an' the money in your traps,' Dan said.

Cord's eyes opened, flicked snake-like from one to the other, as the men spoke.

'Tell us about Vorn.' The sheriff came close, lowered his head, menacingly. 'Tell us.'

'Me an' Vorn had it planned good. We were goin' to buy cheap, when there weren't any more livin' owners. The railroad's runnin' a spur line across the basin. Land would make me as rich as Croesus.'

Dan looked knowingly at Will, as Nitch Gordam leaned in to speak to Cord.

'I got a cousin over at Fort Kearney,' the ranch owner stated. 'He tells me there ain't enough financial gain for the Union an' Central. They changed their minds, Cord. They ain't goin' to run that line.'

At last, the first signs of enragement wrenched at the corners of Cord's eyes and mouth.

'A lot of folk died for your stupid, futile greed, Cord. Your dyin' don't seem enough . . . don't seem much like proper justice.' Elam Medows got so close, the ends of his string tie brushed the dying man's face. His words were angry and vehement.

'Did you ever find out why the night clerk thought Joe Dace had left the Ivy Rooms?' Will asked Hatte, forgetting Cord for the moment.

'Yeah. He found the key to Joe's room on the desk. Figured he'd left without tellin' anybody. Simple assumption, but wrong.'

'Get me the doc,' Cord groaned. His face was pain-filled, doughy, and streaked with sweat. 'Lettin' me die's as good as murder in the eyes o' the law.'

'Of a sudden, you're as poor as Job's turkey, Cord,' Hatte said coldly. 'Elam's right, so we're all passin' your door.'

Now Fearon Chappel had something to say. 'One o' my riders tells me they found Jasper Stebbs's body lyin' out by the wagon road,' he said. '*I* can give you a few reasons, but why the hell would *Cord* have murdered him?'

'He wouldn't have done, an' he didn't,' Dan said. 'At the dealin' end of a Winchester, your foreman wanted me an' Will to move out o' the territory. We didn't want to go.'

Hatte nodded wisely. 'We'll have to talk that through, some time,' he suggested. 'In the meantime, I guess someone's got to move this bloody mess.'

'Yeah, 'cause he won't be needin' the doctor,' Medows said, and dropped the hood back over Cord's lifeless face.

25

THE REWARD

In the dining-room of Ivy's Rooms, the doctor and the townswomen had finished most of their work with the wounded. Most of those helping out had returned home, and the lobby was no longer a waiting room for casualties. Further down the main street a group of people had emptied the water troughs with buckets and bowls. They'd managed to douse the flames of the fires caused by the Blood Legs' attempts at fire-raising.

At the Beaker's Brim saloon, Nestor Midland walked over to the group of men sitting around a poker table.

'You been at my hard-boiled eggs again?' Truckle teased him. 'I told you, no man can eat more'n four.'

'No, no,' the bank manager flustered, and turned to Dan. 'I've been wondering about what you said a little while ago. You mentioned that it was Cord who planted the money and the note in your brother's traps. Yet, when the sheriff and his deputies searched you, they didn't find any trace of it. I was wondering where it was.'

Will actually believed Midland to be an honest man, even if pompous and small-minded. And he didn't like him, wanted to make him pay for his overbearing behaviour.

'There never was any money, Midland,' he said with a straight face. 'Not that got out of anyone else's hands but yours. You an' Cord decided to take a slice, did you?'

Midland's eyes were popping with indignation. 'The very thought of such a thing,' he growled. 'Cord came to see me in the bank today . . . er yesterday, sometime. He said he'd found a packet of money in your saddle-bags. He was sure it was the money stolen from the Harrison bank. I just thought I'd ask about it?'

'Well, *where* is the money, then?' the sheriff asked. 'An' why didn't Cord take it?'

'I guess that's somethin' that only Cord knows,' Will concocted.

Midland tugged at the lapels of his frock coat. 'If it ever turns up, we'll post it on to you. Think of it as a reward for all your help, for the wrong thinking of some of us,' he intoned, with his dignity just about intact.

'That was a long night,' Dan mumbled tiredly, when they were out in the street. 'Can't think of why we'd want to stay here any longer, can you?'

Will looked up at the brightening sky. 'Nope. I can think o' six hundred reasons to go, though.'